I0705480

Other books by Deirdre Hutchins

The Paranormal Investigators League series

PIL #1 Voodoo in Savannah

PIL #2 A Hanging in Tucson

PIL #3 Suicide on Sunset

PIL #4 The Legend of Providence

PIL #5 Darkness in Denver

PIL #6 Spirits in Seattle

PIL #7 Creepy Doll in Detroit

PIL Prequel: The Origin Story

The Dark Prophecy trilogy

1: Resurrection of the Vampire

2: Vengeance of the Damned

3: Deliverance from the Prophecy

The Daphne Winters Psychic Investigation Series

DW1 The Body and the Soul

DW2 Finding Maddy

DW3 Dropped Dead

DW 4 Vanished

These are all available from the San Joaquin Valley Press.

Visit us at www.sanjoaquinvalleypress.com

The Paranormal Mystery Series

Drowned in Portland

Paranormal Investigators League Series #8

A Novel
By Deirdre Hutchins

San Joaquin Valley Press
Fresno, California

Drowned in Portland is published by
     San Joaquin Valley Press
     P.O. Box 9485
     Fresno, CA 93792
     www.sanjoaquinvalleypress.com

Cover design by Andria Davis Kaye
The cover is a collage of elements from Shutterstock:
#2186307841 by Andreiuc88 and #1235224222 by BARAN ARIMAN

ISBN 979-8-9905729-3-5

About Deirdre Hutchins:
Deirdre graduated from Pepperdine University and currently lives in Oregon, where she works as a marketing specialist. When she isn't at her day job, she writes fantasy and ghost stories. She has published 16 books so far and is hard at work on another. Watch for it at the San Joaquin Valley Press website.

Contents

Drowned in Portland

Chapter 1 - The Mellin Family

"Time for lights out, Keenan." Lucy Mellin stood at the doorway of her son's room, hand on the door.

"Mom." Keenan looked up from the comic book he was reading. His disappointment bordered on a meltdown. He'd been getting better as he got older at controlling his emotions, but sometimes they overwhelmed him. Controlled him. He felt the tidal wave waiting to burst onto the shore. "I'm almost done."

Lucy walked over to Keenan and took the comic out of his hands. "Why must you rot your brain with this nonsense?" She put the comic on his nightstand and helped Keenan lay down, tucking him in. "No more tonight. It's time for sleep."

"But, Mom—"

"No buts. Sleep." She pressed her lips to his forehead.

He felt the tears of frustration threatening to fall, but he held them in. He was proud of himself, holding it all together. His mother was none the wiser and it made his chest swell with the accomplishment.

"Good night," Lucy said, turning off the light and blowing another kiss to her nine-year-old son.

Suddenly in the shadow of the hallway, a figure appeared. Lucy screamed at the surprise. "Rachel! What are you doing out of bed?"

Seven-year-old Rachel Mellin stood at her mother's feet with a teddy bear tucked under one arm. "There's a creepy lady outside my window."

Lucy sighed. There was always something with these two. And it always came up at bedtime. How many times had she tried to explain to these kids that one day they wouldn't hate going to bed so much? But, of course, it had fallen on deaf ears.

"Rachel. You have got to stop watching so much YouTube." Lucy turned her young daughter around and aimed her back toward her own bedroom. "Now back to bed with you."

"Will you tell the lady to go away?" Rachel asked, looking up at her mom with hopeful eyes.

"Yes, of course," Lucy answered. *Anything to get you to go to sleep.*

Joe Mellin had to start work at five in the morning and his current construction site was an hour's drive away from Portland. This meant that he had to get to bed early, so he was already snoring softly at the end of the hall. Lucy wasn't bitter about it. She was thankful for his job and the security it was currently providing them. She was just exhausted. It meant she was on her own many nights a week, and she was tired from working her own job as a teacher.

They walked into Rachel's room, and the young girl was kind enough to not put up a fuss. She just climbed into bed.

"She's right out there." Without getting up,

Rachel just gestured to her window.

Lucy pulled the curtain back, not expecting to see anything but figuring it would be smart not to assume. She saw just the tall trees that surrounded their home. It was why she loved this place. Trees all around and just a short hike down the hill to the Tualatin River. Such scenic beauty.

"Go away, Creepy Lady, so Rachel can get some sleep," Lucy sing-songed into the night in an effort to placate her restless daughter.

"Did she listen?" the little girl asked, teddy bear still tucked under the arm that sat above the covers.

Lucy smiled at her little girl. When had she gotten so big? It felt like only yesterday she could barely talk, and now she was reading and writing far beyond her second-grade level. "Yes, she's..."

But when she looked back out, a dark outline of a woman in a long dress stood between the trees. "What is that?" Lucy leaned in to try and make details of what she was seeing. It certainly appeared to be a creepy woman, but she was more like a shadow—just solid black. She stood between the trees looking at the house.

More than seeing, Lucy could *feel* the shadowy woman watching the house.

Rachel sat up. "Did she listen, mommy? Did she go away like you said?"

Letting the curtain fall closed, Lucy turned to her daughter. She tried to appear casual, lest she stir up the very child she was putting to bed. But her heart was pounding in her body, and she felt that anyone was likely to see that, along with the perspiration on her upper lip and her wide, fearful eyes. "Oh, yes, honey. She's gone. Time for you to get some sleep."

Rachel lay back down and had the decency to close her eyes. "Are you sure?"

Lucy kissed Rachel's forehead with a quick peck. "Yep. I'm sure."

But she wasn't really sure, so she double-timed her steps out of Rachel's room and down the hallway to her own bedroom where Joe was fast asleep. They had two large windows in their room and the one over the bed looked onto the side yard. However, the window over the dresser had the same view as in Rachel's room. So she walked straight there and pulled back her own curtain.

And let out a heavy breath. No one was there.

Lucy sat on her bed and put her forehead into her hands. She must be really tired. Or losing it. She admonished herself for allowing her own imagination to take over and get sucked into a child's fantasy.

And yet, her heart was still pounding.

She wasn't crazy, was she? She *had* seen the figure of a woman.

She looked at the clock. It was after ten. Joe's alarm would be going off in five hours, and she'd be lucky if she could continue sleeping. She simply had no more time to deal with kids tonight. She had to get to bed.

Walking into her en suite bathroom, she turned on the softer of the two lights so she didn't risk waking her husband. Letting the water run for a moment or two before grabbing her toothbrush, Lucy stared at her reflection in the mirror.

Despite only being in her thirties, she noticed lines that had never been there before. One lone gray hair bucked the system and forged its own course growing wildly at her temple. Ah, well, only another decade and her kids would be off to college.

It wasn't that she had an especially stressful life. The third-grade class she was teaching this year was generally well-behaved. Her own kids, Rachel and Keenan, were typical for their age. Joe had a unique schedule, but they were happy in their marriage and happy with the money his career was providing.

Overall, she knew she had a lot to be thankful for. There were just certain times when the hecticness of daily life caught up with her, and then out would spring the random gray hair.

She ran her toothbrush across her teeth with a ferocity that was neither necessary nor helpful. Somehow, in her mind, she could brush for less time if she made up for it with great gusto, her end desire being the cozy bed that called to her from the darkness of her bedroom. Joe's gentle snores were luring her like the power of an enchantress.

She spit and rinsed her mouth, taking one final heart-wrenching look in the mirror before wiping her mouth on the nearby towel. A quick costume change into her pajama bottoms and T-shirt and she was able to crawl gently and quietly into bed next to her sleeping husband.

But no sooner had she closed her eyes, than she heard a thud down the hall. Suddenly wide awake and very alert, Lucy sat up in bed and listened intently. Had someone fallen out of bed? Had something somewhere fallen off a shelf? Were the kids putzing around the house when it was way past their bedtime? Even though it danced along the edge of her thoughts, she refused to entertain the notion that there was an intruder.

Until the scream.

There was no mistaking Keenan's cries. Sometimes he screamed in frustration, but this was different. A mother knows that sound better than she knows her own soul. Flying out of bed, she only shouted her husband's name and ran out of the room.

As she hurried down the hall, she saw Rachel standing at Keenan's doorway, teddy bear still tucked beneath her arm.

The little girl turned sad eyes to her mother. "You said she listened. She didn't listen, mom."

Rachel's words made no sense to Lucy, so she ignored her. What does listening have to do with Keenan falling out of bed? But as she joined Rachel at her son's bedroom door, she noticed the empty bed with the sheets pulled back. Her heart began pounding, and it wasn't just from running down the hall. Her mother's intuition was already sounding the alarm bells. Something was desperately wrong.

A glance upward to the open window, no screen, sent her into full blown panic.

"JOE!" The voice that erupted from her chest was so guttural that it didn't even sound like her own. She ran to the open window as Rachel joined her.

"The creepy lady. She took Keenan." The little girl seemed much calmer than her mother felt, although her eyes were wide as she endeavored to understand why anyone would steal her brother from his bed.

Looking into the night, Lucy could see the outline of a woman, her outline blacker than the night itself—as if light were powerless to penetrate her soul. But that wasn't what caught Lucy's eye. What changed everything was the feet hanging from one side of the woman's shadow and the small head on the other side, like she was carrying him babydoll style.

The woman of darkness was carrying Keenan off into the night.

"What's going on?" a groggy Joe asked from Keenan's bedroom door. But Lucy ignored him. Fueled by one thought and one thought only, she climbed through the open window bare feet and all, running into the night after her oldest child.

She'd be damned before she let some strange woman kidnap her child while she stood by and watched.

"The lady took Keenan, daddy," Rachel explained to her father.

It took him a moment to process, and he still had lots of questions, but Joe was Keenan's father just as Lucy was his mother. Less eager to climb out the window, he picked his daughter up into his arms and ran out the front door, following his wife into the night and actually having the awareness to slip on his rain boots before bounding out the front door.

Lucy wanted to scream, but her focus wouldn't let her expend energy on anything but catching up to Keenan.

Every once in a while, the woman of darkness would be swallowed up by trees and Lucy would lose sight of her. It didn't slow Lucy down. She continued running as fast as her bare feet would allow after the woman who had taken her son, dodging formidable evergreens as she went.

The moon was bright overhead, which was a huge blessing because in Portland there was often a haze in the sky that blocked stars and moonlight. Lucy needed it tonight and she silently thanked the universe for this one tiny miracle.

As they hurried through trees down the hill, Lucy realized where they had to be headed. The Tualatin River.

Was she planning to throw him on a boat and traffic him? Was she going to drown him? What was the end game here?

It didn't matter. If they got to the river the stakes would get higher. That was enough to light a fire under Lucy's exhausted limbs. She ran all the harder, following the woman of darkness down the hill, through the trees, and toward the water.

"Lucy!" Joe's voice echoed into the night, coming from behind and then surrounding her.

She couldn't turn around and she couldn't stop. Joe would have to catch up. But she could share what little she knew. "The river!"

And she pushed on.

The river was now in her line of sight at the bottom of a semi-steep drop-off. How on earth the woman carried Keenan over this cliff Lucy had no idea. She had seen her descend over the edge, and Lucy was hell bent on taking the exact same route until she caught up to the woman of darkness.

The only trouble now was the shadowy woman was nowhere to be seen.

"Keenan!" Lucy screamed into the night as her son's body lay below her in the river. He wasn't moving.

Giving zero regard for her own personal well-being, Lucy stepped over the edge of the slight drop-off. And her foot slipped. Falling on her rear end, she slid the remaining way down to the sandy river's edge. Sticks scraped her underside, wedging their way up her sleep shorts. Brush scratched her arms. There were likely twigs in her hair.

And none of that mattered.

She ran into the shallows of the river, the cold water biting her ankles. She ignored the pain as it slowly gave way to numbness. Grabbing Keenan's motionless body, she held him to her chest.

He wasn't breathing.

Lucy's heightened sense of purpose now gave way to pure blown panic. Tears began to fall as she screamed Keenan's name.

Believing in her heart that there was no way he could have drowned that quickly, she pulled him to the sandy shore and began the chest compressions she remembered from decades ago when she had learned CPR.

As Joe, still holding Rachel in his arms, turned around the bend—he clearly had chosen the safer route—Lucy screamed to him, "Call 9-1-1!"

Nothing made any sense. Were they really outside in the middle of the night? Had an outline of a woman really kidnapped their son, who was now not breathing? Had Lucy truly chased the strange apparition down to the river? Surely all of this was some strange nightmare that Lucy would awaken from any moment.

Tears fell from her cheeks and onto Keenan's face as she continued frantically trying to save her child's life. She refused to entertain an outcome any different than the one she willed. The one where Keenan sat up and asked why she was crying.

Joe ran to her side, setting Rachel down next to him in the sandy area near the water's edge. The peaceful sound of the water did nothing to calm the panicked family watching, waiting and hoping as they circled the young boy.

And then, as if Lucy's determination alone could manifest a miracle, Keenan began to cough. He twisted onto his side and coughed up river water. Lucy patted his back, urging him to clear his lungs.

When he was breathing more freely, he looked up at his mother and then collapsed with his arms around her neck. Every member of the Mellin family began to cry tears of fear and relief. And no one voiced what everyone was thinking, lest speaking the words would somehow call the mysterious woman back to finish what she'd started.

Had the Woman of the River, a ghost and local legend, just tried to murder Keenan?

Chapter 2 – A Sunny Day in L.A.

"Good to see you again, Greg!" Duncan beamed as he spoke the words he was surprised to find he actually meant. After their case at the Olive Nightclub in Seattle, Duncan had begun to appreciate Greg a little more and was always happy Paige had found someone special to her.

The orange couch in the window of their favorite coffee shop on Ventura Boulevard creaked under the weight of Duncan's size. Unafraid, Greg grabbed the open seat next to Duncan. Nelson and Duane were already there, seated in chairs across from the leader of their paranormal investigating crew, while Paige was ordering iced coffee drinks for herself and her husband.

"Good to see all of you, as well." Greg nodded to Nelson and Duane while shaking Duncan's hand. Nelson smiled back but Duane ignored his greeting. It was the most kindness he could offer the man. "Paige tells me you guys are headed to Portland, Oregon next."

"Sounds like you know more than we do," Duncan answered, lifting his foot to rest on his knee, his large leg bouncing with boundless energy.

"That's all I know, I swear." Greg laughed nervously, his hands up in mock innocence.

"It's all good, Greg. I know Paige will fill us in on all the details." Duncan rested a gentle but large hand on Greg's shoulder.

"I wonder if our case is related to the Shanghai Tunnels in Portland," Nelson pondered to the team. He sat ramrod straight in his mid-century style chair, hair slicked into place and pastel-colored polo shirt completely wrinkle-free. In fact, the only person in the whole California coffee shop who could compete with Nelson's polish was Paige's husband. Everyone else was in casual beach wear and flip flops. Nelson would never let his toes hang free. "I've been meaning to check those out some time," he continued. "They're famous for active spiritual activity."

"What has spiritual activity?" Paige asked as she came up behind Nelson, a drink in each hand.

"Portland, apparently," Duncan answered. Despite being seated, he barely needed to look up to talk to the standing Paige.

"Oh, yes! Our next case. This is an exciting one, guys." Paige walked around Nelson to squeeze into the small space between Greg and Duncan, handing her husband his drink at the same time she flopped herself onto the couch. "The Mellin family had a really terrifying night not too long ago."

Although she was speaking of a family's horror and suffering, Paige grinned wildly. She would never laugh at the family's fear, but the source of the fear? That's what got this team out of bed in the morning.

"Why don't you fill us in, Paige? What happened to this family and why did they think paranormal?" Duncan asked, his knee still bouncing.

"Is it the Shanghai Tunnels?" Nelson asked hopefully.

"What? No." Paige leaned in. "The Woman in

the River." She sat back and took a sip of her drink. "Or at least that's their theory. That's what they want us to prove, actually."

"Oh, *that* legend!" Nelson nodded thoughtfully. "Also well-known ghost lore in that region."

"So they just want us to look into a local legend? Or did something happen to this family?" Duncan asked again, eyebrow raised. He had done this long enough to know that curious people don't tend to call in professionals. Reinforcements were called in for the terrified.

Paige took another sip and nodded. "Lucy Mellin, the mother, told me that her son Keenan was kidnapped out of his bed at night and taken to the river where the Woman in the River tried to drown their son!" She beamed. At the sight of Duncan's horrified face she waved a hand. "He's fine. The parents got there in time."

"Paige." Duane spoke sternly and sat up from his slouched position. "You need to start asking more qualifying questions. We are not going to Portland to investigate a kidnapping."

"Kidnapped by a ghost, Duane!" Paige responded.

"I'm a little concerned myself, Paige." Duncan rubbed his chin. "What made this family think it was a ghost who kidnapped their child and not just a regular kidnapper?"

"I might be able to shed a little light here," Nelson answered, holding up a finger. "The Woman in the River is like a La Llorona kind of story. Since the earliest white settlers moved to the greater Portland area, there's been a ghost story about a woman who drowned her two children in the river and then flung herself from a bridge. Apparently, she spends her afterlife searching for her own lost children so if she finds one that fits her fancy, she takes them and drowns them in the river so they can be with her for all eternity." At everyone's staring faces, Nelson quickly added. "Or at least that's what the legend says."

"So the minute someone kidnaps your child, you instantly assume it's a ghost if you live in Portland?"

Duane asked skeptically. "I'm not buying it."

"Well, you might if the woman was also a black shadow, floating through the trees as she carried your son down to the river," Paige answered back with a smug look.

"We have to at least go check it out. I mean, a chance at the Woman in the River? This is a great opportunity," Nelson said, smiling at Paige.

But Duncan continued rubbing his chin, a debate warring in his mind. "The last time we were called out to a local legend, no one wanted us to make it go away. Is this just another case of prove-it-and-be-gone? Because I'd rather help people who need it."

But Paige shook her head. "No. This family is terrified and truly believe they witnessed the Woman in the River. And, more importantly, they are really afraid she will try and come back to finish what she started. The little boy, Keenan, hasn't slept in weeks."

"Did the family file a police report?" Greg joined in like he was part of the team. Duncan was open to it, even as Duane just rolled his eyes at Paige's husband.

"I believe they called 9-1-1 and authorities did show up. I don't know that a thorough investigation was done," Paige answered.

Duncan frowned. "I'm not sure, Paige. Kidnapping just doesn't seem like our thing."

Paige shifted in her seat to turn and face her oversized boss. "But helping scared families is. Duncan, please. It's only one state over. We check it out and if there's nothing there, we come home. Easy peasy."

Duncan raised an eyebrow toward his scientific teammate. "Nelson? What do you think?"

With a nod toward the only female in the group, Nelson responded, "I agree with Paige. Legends are born of something, and the family did experience a terrifying event. We owe it to them to at least check it out."

"And you really want to know if the Woman in the River is true." Duane couldn't help but roll his bright blue eyes again.

Nelson looked sheepish. "And there is that."

"I mean, what if, Duncan?" Paige asked with a

hopefulness on her face.

"What if what?" Duncan asked back.

"What if the legend is real and we can solve the Woman in the River? If the legends are real, she's been terrorizing families for a century and a half or more. We'd be helping families in perpetuity!" Paige sat up with the energy that her joy filled her with at the prospect of all the good they could do with this case.

"I think that's likely a stretch," Duncan responded, bringing them all back down to reality.

"I think it's more likely that this is a case for the police," Duane added, again slouching in his seat under his hoodie.

"I think there's no harm in checking it out." Nelson shrugged. "Worst case we lose a couple of days."

"Wanna know what I think?" Greg asked the team.

"Not really," Duane responded.

But Greg ignored him just as Paige would and answered anyway. "I think it's very possible that both things are true. You'll likely have to work *with* the local police on this one."

"Not really our area of expertise," Nelson mentioned.

"They won't even believe us if we find evidence," Duane muttered.

"But Daphne does it all the time. And they completely trust her," Duncan mused. He shrugged as he weighed the opportunity.

Paige took another sip of her iced coffee. "Let's do it, team. We're investigators. They're investigators." Paige again turned toward Duncan, flipping on the pouty face. "The Mellins are a scared family, Duncan. We can't *not* respond."

Duncan frowned again. She had him there. Hadn't he always done this to help people? And ghosts. Helping ghosts find closure was definitely part of the job. He wasn't sure what it was about this case that was nagging at him. Maybe he was worried he'd find a human trafficking ring at the end of all this? They were for sure not equipped to go against something like that.

"I'll say yes on one condition." Duncan held up

his pointer finger to accentuate his requirement.

Paige clapped and bounced on the orange couch. "Anything!"

"Any hint, even the slightest whiff, that we are dealing with something non-paranormal and we are out of there. A kidnapping ghost I'll deal with. Regular kidnappers? We're outta there." Duncan shook his head at Paige.

"Deal!" Paige squealed.

"I think that's more than fair," Nelson added, nodding in agreement.

Without sitting up or changing his body language in any way to show he was engaged with the conversation, Duane said flatly, "At least the food is good in Portland."

Chapter 3 - The Tualatin River

"Why do people live here?" Duane groaned as they parked the white P.I.L. van in front of the address Paige had given them. The sky was gray and moisture drizzled on the windshield. "It's depressing."

"My guess is that." Nelson pointed up at the tall evergreen trees that blanketed the background. "I find the nature to be invigorating."

Duane emitted a sound somewhere between a groan and a grunt, but otherwise he sat there in silence.

Nelson started to open the door, saying, "Should we go talk...?"

But that was as far as he got before Duane grabbed his arm. "I don't talk to clients."

Nelson shut the door with a slam. He was starting to get more and more confident with the people who called them out to investigations, but he had enough self-awareness to know that he couldn't do it by himself.   He started tapping on the window with nervous energy, couped up in the van waiting—as usual—for Paige and Duncan to appear in Duncan's barely-running old Chevy.

It was sometimes a miracle to Nelson that when he looked at the undercarriage, he didn't see Duncan's feet as the force that powered the vehicle. But he knew that Duncan's philosophy was never to fix something that wasn't broken. Duncan's car, as old and slow as it was, was still able to get him places all around the country. The engine would probably have to implode on itself before Duncan entertained the very idea of getting a new one.

And getting a new one most likely consisted of replacing this old car with another old car, just newer old.

That was Duncan's style. He'd lived in the same ratty old apartment with cockroaches in the San Fernando Valley that he had lived in since he'd moved out of his parents' house. Drove the same old rundown car. Probably was wearing the same raggedy jeans from high school.

The only thing he ever spent any money on was equipment to help them get better at investigating ghosts and the paranormal.

"Stop that," Duane grunted at Nelson, who took his hand down from the window immediately.

And then he began rubbing his khaki pants instead. "Who do you think La Llorona really is?"

Duane snorted. "I think it's probably a bunch of horse shit."

"But so many cultures have a lady-of-the-water type story. Doesn't that seem to you like there might be something there? It can't be collective hallucinations across time and space."

"Nelson." Duane turned his bald head and stared his bright blue eyes at his co-investigator. "Every city in every generation has at least one thing in common: parents who want to scare their children straight."

Nelson nodded, conceding that Duane's theory could be a possibility. "I've thought of that too. Lots of cultures have threats of a creature that will carry naughty children off into the night, like Krampus. But I do believe that people could be extraordinarily afraid of the ghosts of women who drowned. It's like the water adds some special mystique or something."

"You know I believe in the ghosts of women who've drowned." Duane leaned his head back against the headrest and crossed his arms. "And we've had some violent ghosts. Ghosts who've thrown us, pushed us, scratched us. But kidnapping? I think that's a stretch."

"We've seen some evil spirits do some fantastical things to try to maintain their power in the afterlife," Nelson responded with a shrug. "I'm going to stay open-minded about the Woman in the River."

"You're always open-minded, Nelson. But what if the family is wrong?"

Nelson cocked his head to the side in question. "How do you mean?"

"Are you here for the Woman in the River? Or for the Mellins?" Duane asked.

Nelson paused for only a moment. "The Mellins, of course." He turned to stare out the window as he added, "But I wouldn't say no to a chance to investigate the legend too."

"That's what I thought." Duane shook his head.

"They're finally here," Nelson announced as he caught a glimpse of Duncan's old car coming up the residential road.

"One day I'm going to disconnect his spark plugs so he's forced to get a new car," Duane muttered.

"You wouldn't." Nelson was shocked at Duane's threat, but as he looked at Duane's deadly serious face, he realized that a gentle nudge isn't always a bad thing. "But it's actually not a half-bad idea."

"Duncan is a huge guy, so sometimes it takes a lot of heavy movement to get him going, but once he does, he usually starts to roll with it."

Nelson nodded and pointed at Duane as he responded, "Roll. Car. I like what you did there."

Before Duane could retort, Duncan rapped on Nelson's window, prompting him to roll it down.

"Paige and I will go connect with the client. You guys wanna come with?" Duncan leaned two elbows on the window frame.

"Not even a little bit," Duane muttered and slouched further in the driver's seat.

"I'll go." Nelson climbed out and pulled up his hood. It was only drizzling, but he didn't want any moisture to touch his hair and make it frizz. Duncan, on the other hand, was in a T-shirt, jeans and flip-flops. No hood in sight.

"Aren't you cold?" Nelson asked when he saw Duncan's Los Angeles attire.

"Yeah. I actually am a little bit." But Duncan kept walking toward the front door where Paige was standing in a light rain slicker. Apparently, he wasn't cold enough to do anything about it. Nelson cringed when Duncan stepped straight into a stream of mud that had begun to ooze onto the walkway. His flip-flop stuck for a moment and then snapped back to his foot when it finally broke free, making a sucking noise followed by a slap as mud splattered all over his bare feet and the back of his jeans.

Duncan kept walking, seemingly oblivious. Nelson just shook his head and then carefully sidestepped the mud altogether.

"Isn't this beautiful? It's like we're in a fairy garden or something." Paige beamed as she spoke to Nelson, all three of them gathered on the doorstep.

Nelson nodded in response. "The forest makes for a stunning backdrop."

Save for a pop of color on the flower bushes out front, it was as if an artist had rendered the home as part of a monochromatic presentation. The trees were darker green. The grass was a brighter green. The Mellins' home was painted a sage green. Green, green, green.

Paige lifted her hand to knock on the dark front door, but it opened before she could touch knuckle to wood.

"Oh, thank God!" The woman standing before them was very typical of the clients who called. She was mid-thirties, hair neatly pulled back in a ponytail, brightly colored sweater with a long skirt. But her wild frantic eyes looked like every terrified client they'd ever worked with.

"Sounds like you realize we're with the Paranormal Investigators League?" Paige asked.

"I honestly don't know how much longer we could afford to live like this. Come in." Lucy Mellin waved the investigators into her home and guided them to the living room couch. "Joe and I haven't worked in weeks because we are too scared to let the kids out of our sight. We're all traumatized by what happened."

"Can you walk us through what happened that night? I'm Duncan, by the way." In his best attempt to be comforting, Duncan smiled a friendly smile.

"Hi, Duncan," Lucy said, nodding, a small half-smile on her face. It was clear she was someone who was patient and kind, but who was needing to force her tiny bit of decorum in this particular case. "I'm Lucy Mellin."

"And I'm Paige and this is Nelson." Paige thumbed an indication at her co-investigator so that all the necessary introductions were now complete.

"Nice to meet you all. Truly." At this, Lucy actually heaved a heavy sigh, as if she could finally hand the smallest piece of the weight she'd been carrying to this group of people. "It was past ten on a school night, so the kids and Joe, my husband, were already in bed. He works in construction in Corvallis, so he has to get up early to make it to his site on time. I had just climbed into bed when I heard a thud and a scream. Rachel, our youngest, told me the lady had taken him, but the words didn't make any sense until I looked out the window and saw it for myself. The Woman in the River had stolen my son from his bed!"

Lucy Mellin was ashen white as she recounted the horrific events.

"How do you know it was the Woman in the River?" Duncan had to ask.

"It was just like they always say. Stories I had always thought were lore and hogwash until now." Lucy leaned in and rubbed her nervous hands on her pants. "She was black. I'm talking blacker than a shadow, as if she were a walking black hole. And it was clearly the outline of a woman, complete with a dress and a figure. She was holding my son like a ragdoll." Lucy lifted an arm as she pointed toward the bedrooms. "And she carried him down to the Tualatin River."

"You followed, I take it?" Nelson asked.

Lucy nodded and then turned to show the team the back of her arms covered in the still-healing wounds. "This is where I fell down the hill as I was chasing them. When I got to the bottom of the hill, she was gone and Keenan was in the river, not breathing."

Paige had to console this trauma-exhausted woman. "Oh, Lucy. That's such an awful experience."

"I have to ask, Lucy. How do you know that it was the Woman in the River and not just some weird lady trying to steal your son?" Duncan asked, rubbing his chin.

"I know it sounds crazy." Lucy shook her head. "I thought I *was* crazy, believe me. But she floated all the way down to the river. And she was absent any light or color. And both those things match the stories people tell. And both those things were not what you'd expect if someone was trying to just terrorize us with some cruel prank."

"Your experience is frightening, no matter what it turns out to have been. We don't think you're crazy at all," Paige explained.

"How hard would those things be to fake, Nelson?" Duncan asked his educated investigator.

Nelson frowned. "The color maybe not so much, but floating all the way down to the river would be very difficult to hoax."

Duncan turned back to Lucy. "And when you say 'floated,' how high off the ground are we talking?"

Lucy shook her head. "It wasn't much. More like she was on a people-mover or something. There were no steps involved as she glided down to the river."

"I'm the biggest skeptic there is," Joe suddenly chimed in from where he leaned against the wall in the living room entry way. "I think people make up a lot of nonsense to help them cope with things they don't understand. Never have believed in ghosts. No offense."

Duncan shook his head. "None taken. You'd be surprised how often we hear that from a client. Quickly followed by a 'but'."

Joe nodded. "But...she was not a human woman. I don't know what she was necessarily, but she wasn't normal."

Lucy cleared her throat. "Perhaps we should show them the drop-off near the river."

"We definitely want to see everything, but why is the drop-off so important that we see?" Duncan asked.

"When you see it, it will make sense. She was carrying Keenan and she never slowed. I fell on my butt with just me by myself. It's impossible to go that way *and* carry a child," Lucy explained.

Joe pushed off the wall he was leaning on and joined them in the living room. "And when you see Keenan, you'll be even more impressed. He's a solidly built nine-year old boy."

"Has Keenan explained how she got in?" Paige had to ask. "Did she come in through the same window she carried him out?"

Lucy shook her head. "I don't know that. I don't know if anyone does."

"Would you be comfortable if we met your kids?" Duncan asked. "I know they're both a little shell-shocked from the experience."

"If you're not a ghost trying to steal them from their beds, I think you'll be okay." Joe huffed a laugh but there was no mirth in it.

Duncan half-smiled in return. He knew perfectly well how life-defining it was to have a supernatural experience as a small child.

Lucy stood. "Follow me. I'll take you to the kids and show you the room where Keenan used to sleep."

Paige and Duncan exchanged a look at the words 'used to sleep.' That was never pleasant to hear, nor unusual, that the one place in the world that should be a sanctuary had become a nightmare.

"I have to ask," Nelson said, clearing his throat. "Have you guys had any other experiences in this house? Like was this the culmination of other paranormal experiences or anything?"

"No, nothing." Lucy began to walk down the hallway, gesturing for the investigators to come along. "Nothing before or since. Just that one terrifying night."

"And it was enough," Joe piped up from the rear.

"So it's definitely not a classic haunted house." Nelson looked at Duncan and adjusted his glasses.

Duncan shook his head as they rounded the corner in the hallway. "Doesn't sound like it. Maybe the land is cursed?"

"Or the river," Paige added.

"Or neither." Nelson frowned as they walked into Joe and Lucy's bedroom.

"You don't think there's a curse? Or what?" Duncan asked, hands on his hips while the two Mellin children played on the floor at their feet.

"She could have cursed herself when she murdered her children in the first place," Nelson said.

Paige rolled her eyes and gestured to the small children who had immediately frozen at Nelson's words. "Little ears, gentlemen."

"It's just a theory," Nelson answered.

"These are our kids, Rachel and Keenan." Lucy introduced her kids while pulling on her son's arm. "Keenan, can you stand for these fine investigators?"

Without asking questions, the young boy obeyed his mother. Duncan was impressed at his fine manners.

"May I stand too, mommy?" the little girl, Rachel, asked.

"Of course, honey," Lucy responded with almost a laugh.

"Well, you two are just such amazing kids." Duncan knelt on one knee to make himself loom less large. Especially compared to Rachel, it wasn't working.

"Why are you so big?" Rachel asked.

Duncan could hear Paige giggling as he responded, "I don't know. I guess I just ate all my vegetables."

"Are you going to make the bad lady go away?" Keenan asked with fear in his eyes.

"That's what we're here to try and do," Duncan answered back. "Are you comfortable sharing what happened to you that night?"

The little boy looked up at his mother before deciding. At her nod, he was satisfied in his decision to open up.

"Well, I was in bed, trying to go to sleep," the little boy began. "I don't know how she got in but suddenly she was in my room."

"What did she look like?" Nelson asked.

"She was solid black, like a shadow. Except I could see a black veil over her head."

"Any facial features?" Duncan added.

Keenan shook his head. "No. Looking at her was like looking into a dark corner of your room."

"What did you do when you saw her?" Paige asked.

"I tried to run. I was trying to get to my mom and dad."

"But you didn't make it?" Duncan assumed.

"I fell when I got out of bed and then I was stunned."

"When you say 'stunned,' what do you mean by

that?" Nelson asked. It was not what they expected to hear.

"Like she got me with a stun gun. You know, like this." At his words, Keenan made himself go rigid, eyes rolling into his head.

"So you were frozen and couldn't move?" Paige asked with awe and wonder.

The little boy nodded. "After that, the next thing I remember was coughing by the river and the paramedics came."

Duncan turned to Rachel. "What about you, little one? Did you have any experiences?"

Rachel shook her head and in a small voice answered, "She was staring in my window all night from the forest. When I heard Keenan fall, I ran to him. I knew the bad lady didn't go away. I just knew it! And there she was in his room."

Duncan looked up at Lucy. "Staring in your windows?"

Lucy nodded. "I can show you where I saw her."

Duncan looked at Paige. Everyone had seen the

creepy shadow lady.

The investigators followed Lucy over to her bedroom window, the one that overlooked the forest. "There." She pointed straight back. "Between those trees."

"Okay, we're definitely going to need to get back there with the equipment," Duncan replied.

"Other than Keenan's bedroom, I don't think any of the investigation needs to be done in this house," Nelson added.

"You think Keenan was a random selection?" Duncan asked his co-investigator.

Nelson shrugged. "Or he was singled out, but I don't know that it's tied to the house at all."

Paige cleared her throat. "Little ears, guys."

"Let me show you Keenan's room." Lucy walked out of her room and the kids went back to playing on the floor. As the investigators followed the mother, Joe again took up the rear. He wasn't adding much to the conversation, but he was hovering as if he needed to be protecting his family at all times. Poor guy probably hadn't slept a wink since the incident.

Lucy turned into a room a couple doors down the hall.

There was nothing unusual about the room. It looked like a typical little boy's room, with blue paint and sports memorabilia on the walls. A comic book rested on the nightstand and there was even dirty laundry littering the floor. A few more items scattered everywhere and it would have reminded Duncan exactly of his childhood room.

"Oh, Night Scavengers. I love this comic!" Duncan bee-lined for Keenan's prized possession. He flipped through the pages with a smile on his face.

"Yes. Keenan loves comic books, but that one does seem to be his favorite. In fact, he was reading it not long before he was taken." Lucy sighed but more so at the dark turn their lives had taken and less at the concern for her son's brain melting from reading too many comic books. That had been a concern *before* the event.

Now it seemed almost ludicrously

inconsequential.

Placing the comic back down on the nightstand, Duncan peered out the window. "So, she's watching all night from the tree line. Then suddenly she's in his room and she takes him down to the river."

"That's right," Lucy affirmed.

"It does sound like she was targeting him," Nelson said.

"Or at least targeting this house," Paige added.

Duncan turned back around. "Yeah. The question is why."

"Maybe her children who died were little boys?" Lucy shrugged and then shook her head. "I don't know, it's just that the stories about the Woman in the River are always that she is looking for her own children that she lost."

Nelson nodded. "That she herself drowned."

Lucy looked nervous, staring at the ground. "That's right."

"So, she drowns more boys to bring back her own boys she drowned?" Duncan raised an eyebrow.

"Doesn't make much sense."

Nelson just shrugged.

Paige gestured toward Nelson and then responded, "We can research the origins of the legend tomorrow."

Lucy nodded enthusiastically. "I'd like to know more about her too."

Duncan turned toward his client. "So, there's no part of you who believes this was an actual live woman who kidnapped your child?"

Lucy shook her head. "Let me take you out to the river and you can see for yourself how unlikely that would be."

Duncan held a hand out. "Lead the way."

Lucy led the investigators out a sliding glass door that framed a dining room near the room they had originally been sitting in. Joe stayed behind this time, presumably to protect his children.

The rain had picked up slightly and was now heavy enough to be called sprinkles. Lucy, Nelson and Paige all put their hoods up. Duncan just shook his head every so often to send the rain drops flying off his long curly hair. His flip-flops punctuated every step with the slap of the heel hitting his foot. When they reached the tree line, Lucy spared a glance at his feet but said nothing.

So Paige answered the unasked question. "Duncan doesn't have a large array of shoe wear."

"I brought boots if it starts raining," Duncan added.

Paige laughed. "What do you call this?"

"Sprinkles."

Lucy joined Paige in laughing and then said, "If this doesn't bother you, you'll be fine. We're not expecting any storms." She then turned to the trees they were standing between. "This is where we saw the shadow lady watching the house. She would've been standing right about here."

Duncan turned back toward the house where he could clearly see the windows. But the distance was decently far, such that he doubted anyone could see inside without binoculars or some sort of assistance.

"And she was watching you?"

"She was staring toward the house," Lucy responded. "And then once she had Keenan, she ran with him through these trees toward the river this way."

Without waiting to be sure they were all following, Lucy turned and headed toward the river. They followed a dirt trail with foliage all around their feet and trees surrounding them in a canopy of nature. Other than the dark reason they were there, Duncan felt a sense of wonder and beauty in this short hike.

Lucy stopped suddenly and the investigators had to brake hard in order not to fall at the edge. "This is where she carried Keenan down to the river."

Duncan let out a long, slow whistle. "This is very steep."

"Where do people normally cut down to the river? Not here, I suppose?" Paige asked.

Lucy shook her head. "Not normally. Because you end up like me." She again held up her arms to indicate where she'd been injured, although the wounds themselves were covered with her sleeves. She then pointed off to the left where her husband and Rachel had joined her at the riverfront that fateful night. "That's the path that leads you down to the water."

"I'm going to try it," Duncan announced.

"In flip-flops?!" Lucy couldn't hide her shock.

But Nelson grabbed his arm to stop him. "I don't think you need to risk injury. I think it's obvious that carrying a small child and climbing down this steep hill would be difficult."

"I might even say impossible," Paige added.

Lucy frowned. "So now you see. This is why I think the Woman in the River tried to murder my son."

Chapter 4 - Investigation in the Trees

"I'm not sitting out in the rain." Duane stated the facts as he stood at the tree line holding an armful of computers and monitoring equipment.

"I think it makes sense for someone to be in the child's room anyway. Just in case." Duncan gestured back toward the house and Duane grunted in response.

"I can show you, Duane." Paige bounced and smiled. "Just make sure to document any experiences you have." At Duane's eyeroll, Paige added, "You aren't usually located in the primary location of an event."

"Just show me where to go."

As Paige and Duane headed back to the Mellin house, Duncan and Nelson continued planning the investigation.

"I think someone should be down by the river." Duncan gestured in the direction of the Tualatin River.

Nelson nodded and said, "I agree. What do you

think about putting someone at the bridge?"

Duncan raised an eyebrow. "The family didn't have any experiences at the bridge." It was a statement that somehow ended up also being a question.

"Well, the Woman in the River legend says she threw herself from a bridge. I don't know that it's *that* bridge, per se..." Nelson let his sentence drift off. Even he wasn't quite convinced.

Duncan chewed his lip for a second and ran his fingers through his long, curly bangs. "Then let's hold off until after you and Paige research the legend. I think it makes sense to investigate her bridge, but I don't want someone a mile away in the dark at possibly the wrong bridge."

Nelson didn't argue. "So the question becomes, are two of us here where the woman watched the house? Or are two of us at the river where she left Keenan to drown?"

Duncan scratched his head in thought. "I think here. If she was here for some extended period of time, then I'm thinking more residual energy would be here than the river."

"And technically, one person could be a floater, walking through the trees and such," Nelson added.

With a clap, Paige announced her return. "And where do you want me?"

"I'm going to head down to the river," Duncan responded. "You and Nelson investigate here among the trees."

Paige looked at Duncan's feet and then tightened her lips in judgment. "Duncan. Please go get actual shoes. I don't want you in these elements in flip-flops."

"And maybe a sweatshirt," Nelson added. "I doubt it will get dryer as the night goes on."

Duncan looked at his feet and then his T-shirt, which was already moderately damp from the drizzle that had been steadily in the air since they arrived in Portland. "No arguing with logic! I'll be back. You guys get ready. I'll use the handheld by the river."

As Duncan flipped and flopped back toward the Mellin home, Nelson began setting up the tripod. "I think I'll aim toward the house, so I at least have the line of sight of the strange woman."

Paige nodded. "All right. I'll aim toward the forest in case she wanders these parts at night searching for victims." They worked in silence for a bit before Paige asked, "What do you think the chances are that she is actually tied to this land?"

Nelson adjusted his glasses. "What do you mean?"

Paige shrugged. "Well. The legend is tied to Portland. Or to the river. Not really to a particular house or forest." Paige looked off into the thick covering of trees before her. "I guess I don't know if I believe she's tied to this land in any way."

"I don't know either, but we have to start somewhere." Nelson aimed his camera and lined up his shot. "I see Duncan in the camera now."

"Can you zoom in and make sure he has shoes?" Paige scoffed.

"He does. He even has a hood!"

Paige laughed. "You're all like children

sometimes, I swear."

Nelson dropped his jaw in mock offense. "All of us?"

"In your own ways, yes. Even you, Nelson." Paige smiled at him gently. "It's true I don't have to remind you to wear shoes or pick up your clothing from the floor. But where's your cell phone?"

Nelson patted his pockets before saying, "I don't need it. I'm here with you."

Paige just shook her head. "As long as each of us does our part, I suppose. It's what makes us a good team."

"Ta-da!" Duncan opened his arms wide and turned a three-sixty. "Am I now ready for a Portland evening, hunting ghosts by the river?"

"At least you have reduced the likelihood that you'll die of pneumonia." Nelson nodded to his friend.

"I think it was rhetorical, Nelson." Paige smiled to herself as she continued adjusting her camera angle.

"I'm heading down." Duncan began walking directly through the trees toward the steep drop-off that Lucy Mellin had shown them earlier in the evening.

"Go the long way, please," Paige instructed Duncan, accentuating her words with a finger pointing toward the safe way down to the river.

In response, Duncan lifted his foot. "I have boots."

"Duncan. Who's going to pick you up if you fall and injure yourself?" Paige stood with her hands on her hips and her head tilted down in a motherly way.

With a heavy sigh, Duncan admitted defeat. He couldn't resist Paige's tone. Or logic. He turned toward the long and safe route.

Paige turned back to her camera. "Children. I'm telling you."

"We don't have any lights to turn off, so I'm just going to begin." Nelson turned his camera on and watched his footage of the house reflected on the screen.

"Same." Paige copied her co-investigator, only her view was of the trees. The sun set later here in the Pacific Northwest than Paige was used to in California, so the sky was a royal blue despite the late hour. But even though there was still a twinge of light in the sky, the trees still felt ominous. They created a wall of mystery, as if walking between two of them allowed you to enter a different world.

Wolves or coyotes could be hiding and watching. Ghosts of prior victims could still be lurking in the shadows. Women who preyed on small children and kidnapped them from their beds could be plotting.

"Is it just me, or do the woods seem scarier than any haunted house we've ever investigated?" Paige asked.

Nelson stood up and turned to look behind himself, staring deep into the forest as if answers to Paige's question would be answered by the trees themselves.

"Probably because it feels so vast. A house is contained. The ghost is localized. Out here..." Nelson let his words trail off with a shrug.

"She could be anywhere, coming at us from any direction," Paige finished Nelson's sentence, her voice softer than normal, as if the Woman in the River might be listening.

"I don't think we have any reason to be afraid. We're not her target market." Nelson turned back to his camera to watch his footage. "She drowns kids."

Paige huffed a laugh. "That doesn't make anything better."

As Duncan marched down the path that took him the long way, he could hear Paige and Nelson's conversation slowly getting quieter and quieter. When the ground got flat and sandy, he headed straight for the river. He sat on his haunches and let his fingers gently graze the water.

It was icier than he expected, making his fingertips go numb, but somehow feeling good at the same time. He looked up all around him and saw nothing but trees and the river as far as the eye could see. Around the river bend he knew there was a bridge, but from where he sat it felt like he was alone in nature.

And he found that it soothed his soul.

He wasn't sure if he would see the shadowy lady

who haunted and terrorized the Mellin family. For once, he wasn't entirely sure he cared. Ghost or not, he was enjoying his evening. A haunting would just be the cherry on top.

He powered up the handheld and panned along the river.

"Hello?" he called out.

The sound of the river was the only response. He slowly started walking along the river's edge, following its natural path toward the direction where the Mellin family said they had found Keenan half-drowned. He panned his camera this way, then that.

And then the sound of crunching behind him. The hair on his neck stood up.

He swung the camera as he turned toward the sound. Was something watching him in the bushes near the base of the hill?

He stepped slowly and carefully, trying as best he could to not make any sound with his enormous feet and heavy build. He kept the camera trained on the bush where the crunching sound was originating as he stepped closer, slowly, easily. One step. Another.

When he was directly above the bush he zoomed in and saw a raccoon busily hoarding his pile of trash, stashing it in the storage container that was the bush.

"Hey there, little guy." Again, he bent down just as he had at the river's edge, only this time he wasn't met with serenity. The raccoon turned and hissed at him. "Well. Fine, then."

He knew Duane was probably really getting a kick out of seeing a raccoon getting feisty with him back in the Mellins' house, so even if they never saw a ghost, he would always have this. Standing back up, he continued his trek along the river's edge.

"Hello?" It was too far in the distance to hike there, but he knew there was a bridge in the general direction he was walking, and the legend of the Woman in the River was about a woman who jumped from a bridge. It was just a hunch, but he thought that could be a more likely place to catch footage of the mysterious black shadow woman.

This was their process and he trusted it, but suddenly he did feel like the tables were turned a bit on them. They knew hardly anything but a few sentences about this legend. Who was she? Why was she kidnapping children in the middle of the night? None of it seemed to make any sense.

"Is there anyone out here who wants to make contact?" Duncan panned left and right, then he slowly swung the handheld camera around toward the trees, panning the forest. The sky was getting darker and darker, forcing more shadows between the trees. It didn't seem too far-fetched that a shadow figure could be hidden in the forest and watching him. He watched back with the camera, trying to shake off the heavy feeling of someone with eyes on him. He saw nothing but darkness in the distance, but Duncan knew that that didn't mean anything at all.

A ghost could very well be lurking between two trees, and he wouldn't be able to see it.

"Can I help you?"

Duncan startled at the sound of the voice from

behind him. "Oh, you scared me. I had convinced myself a ghost was watching me from the tree line."

The old man and his golden retriever were almost caught up to him. He smiled with kindness in his eyes. "Go get it, James!" And then he threw a ball into the dark distance, and his dog ran after it at full speed.

"Your dog is named James? Never heard that one before."

The old man bent down as James the Golden ran back with the ball in his mouth. "James Dean, actually. We've just always called him James. For short."

"Huh. I like that. A throwback classic."

"Not to pry, but may I ask what you're doing out here in the dark talking to no one and worrying about ghosts?" The old man gestured toward the camera in Duncan's hand.

"Oh, this?" He held his hand out and the man shook it. "Paranormal Investigators League. I'm Duncan, by the way."

"Carl. Nice to meet you. Paranormal, huh? Someone worried about a river ghost?"

"Actually, yes. The Woman in the River. I've heard she's well known in these parts."

Carl let out a long, slow whistle and then threw the ball again. James ran full speed after it. "Boy is she ever. She's like the Portland Boogey Man. But I think she is closer to the city or something. Never heard much about her out this way and I've lived here all my life."

"We have a family just over this hill who thinks they may have had an encounter with her." Duncan pointed in the direction of the Mellin family home.

Carl rubbed his chin in response. "Near the Tualatin? Huh. I figured the rumors were about the Willamette."

"What's that?" Duncan asked.

"That's one of the other rivers near here. Heads toward the city. A much bigger river, to be honest." James the Golden ran back to his owner and dropped the ball at his feet.

"Is that why you assumed the rumors were associated with the other river and not this one?" Duncan asked, still filming. He didn't want to find out later there was a ghost the whole time and he had just been distracted talking to this man.

"No, not so much because of the size. Just all the rumors seemed to be happening somewhere else. You know how stories and rumors are." Carl picked up the ball and threw it again. "Lots of details and yet no specifics at all of the kind that truly matter."

"What specifics have you heard?" Duncan watched as James, yet again, grabbed the ball and ran back at full speed. He seemed to be as happy as a dog could be, chasing a ball in the late evening darkness down by the river.

"Well, they'll talk about things like how she wears a long dress and had two kids she drowned, but who she was exactly and where she drowned those kids no one really seems to know." Carl knelt down and gave James a good rub behind the ears.

"Do you believe what you've heard?" Duncan had to ask.

Carl seemed to think about it for a moment before answering. "I don't *not* believe it. Honestly, I never really thought about it much one way or the other. As a teenager and young adult, it came up at parties and such, like a way to scare one another. But in my daily life? Don't much talk about a supposed ghost haunting rivers."

Carl stood up, putting James's ball in his pocket, thereby ending the play time. And then he pointed at Duncan's camera again. "Caught anything so far?"

Duncan looked at his camera. "Not that I know of. Honestly, it's been pretty quiet. But that doesn't mean anything necessarily."

"Well, I gotta be getting home, but I actually do hope you find some real information about her."

"Why is that, may I ask?" Duncan asked.

"If we really do have a ghost that haunts the river and kidnaps children, I'd like to know about it. And also, I'd like her spirit to find peace. No one should be going through eternity reliving the worst day of their lives." Carl shook his head and frowned.

"What did you say?" Duncan had wondered about her need to kidnap children, but Carl was presenting a theory Duncan had never thought about before.

"I feel bad for the ghost. It might sound weird to say, but..."

"No, I mean after that. About reliving her worst day. What's that about?" Duncan pressed.

Carl shrugged. "I'm not a paranormal investigator or anything. You're the professional. Just that the rumors say she drowned her kids and jumped off a bridge. And now she spends her afterlife, supposedly, committing her atrocities over and over again. Like some kind of punishment."

Duncan chewed on his lip. Sometimes they dealt with curses their ghost had started, but sometimes they themselves were victims. "That's an interesting theory."

"Will you help her?" Carl asked. "If you find out the truth, can you help her find peace?"

Duncan nodded. "That's the idea. Yes."

"I like that." Carl patted Duncan's arm. "Then I certainly wish you good luck. Nice meeting you, Duncan."

"Likewise! Nice meeting you, Carl." Duncan smiled in the dim light of the evening. He had truly enjoyed talking to Carl.

Another whistle from Carl and James ran to his side as they walked back the way they came. Duncan watched them leave for a moment before focusing again on his investigation. He made a mental note to talk to the team about the idea of the Woman in the River being forced to relive her awful last day over and over for all eternity.

That did seem like a very specific type of hell.

But for now, Duncan panned across the river where a shadow seemed to be forming. He couldn't make out what it was from the distance in the dark, but it felt heavy.

And, again, he couldn't shake the eerie feeling that he was being watched.

Chapter 5 - The Legend Behind the Legend

Duane was the last to come down the stairs and meet his team in the lobby of the hotel. Despite the fact they were indoors and the rain had stopped outside anyway, his hoodie was up and covering his bald head.

"Good morning, Sleeping Beauty." Paige smiled and waved at Duane, and he grunted in response.

"I can't shake it. What Carl told me. What if everyone has had it wrong and the Woman in the River is just as much a victim as the families she torments?" Duncan ran his fingers through his long bangs, just as he always did when he was deep in thought.

"Interesting theory, for sure." Nelson adjusted his glasses. "Perhaps she's cursed."

"She could be haunted herself, I suppose," Paige added, nodding along with Duncan and Nelson.

"Who cares?" Duane snorted.

Paige put her hand to her heart in mock shock.

"We do. It's our job, Duane."

"No. Our job is to get peace for the family. Our job is the same whether she *is* the curse or she is *because* of a curse." Duane folded his arms.

"Huh." Duncan scratched his nose. "I don't know if that's true. I mean, I definitely want to help the Mellins. But I want to help the Woman in the River too. Regardless of her origin."

"Yes, of course." Nelson folded his hands in his lap. "We always help the ghosts."

Duane just grunted again in acknowledgment.

"Well, I can certainly head to the library and see what I can find out about the woman behind the legend, but I think someone should also interview more locals. There could be something we're missing so far." Paige sat back with a smile.

Duncan pointed at Paige. "Great idea. Nelson and I will hit the streets with the handheld. Duane? I assume you'll continue watching footage?"

Duane stared at Duncan before answering. "I'm not talking to locals, that's for sure."

Duncan clapped his hands together. "Then it's settled. We can regroup around four to share what we have so far with the Mellin Family."

"I don't suppose you've seen anything so far on the footage from last night?" Nelson asked Duane, who just shook his head in response.

"It was pretty quiet." Paige frowned.

Duncan leaned in and shook his head. "I don't know. Looking into the dense tree line... It felt like something was watching me. The whole time."

"I do wish we had trees like that back home. There's no mystery in big buildings and bright lights of the city," Paige responded.

"That's just your imagination," Nelson explained. "It fills in the answers, like a Rorschach test. You and I both know there are just as many mysteries in buildings as there are in nature."

"If there are people, there are ghosts," Duncan announced, standing up as if that were the final answer. "We'll meet back here at four."

Duane stood and silently returned the way he

had just come moments ago, back to the stairs and to his room to watch footage. Silently. With no one talking to him. Just the way he liked it.

Paige lifted her over-sized purse onto her shoulder. "I'm off to the library. If I learn anything cool, I'll fill you in."

Duncan nodded. "Likewise."

"Bye, Paige." Nelson raised his hand in a wave that never quite made it to the crest.

"Let's go ask the front desk where we should head. Carl had said he thought the river she drowned in was a different river." Without waiting for a response, Duncan turned and marched across the hotel lobby.

"It's good to go where people are knowledgeable about the legend for sure, but I doubt it matters much where she died."

Duncan stopped so suddenly that Nelson bumped into his shoulder. "It doesn't matter where she died?"

Nelson adjusted his glasses in emphasis to his nod. "Water is very powerful. It's also very fluid. She can likely travel along it just as someone haunting a train isn't tied to one train station." A shrug. "It's just a theory."

"Huh." Duncan rubbed his chin. "Decades of experience and this case is blowing all conventional wisdom to bits."

"We have to think of them as themes, so we know how to approach it and systematically handle it. But each and every case is unique and distinct."

"I hope we find the Woman in the River." Duncan clapped his hands together in glee and wiggled his eyebrows. "So we can ask her."

"That would be ideal," Nelson agreed.

When Duncan made it to the front desk, he leaned across the desk as if holding up the top half of his body was just too great a weight to bear. A quick glance at the name tag worn by the woman behind the counter and then, "Excuse me, Marie."

Marie smiled, seemingly unflustered by Duncan's casual stance and closeness. "How can I help you?"

Duncan angled a thumb at Nelson as he spoke. "If we were wanting to know more about the Woman in the River legend, where do you think we should head? Like, to talk to locals who may know the back story?"

If Marie thought this was a strange request, she never faltered. A picture-perfect model of hospitality with her dark hair pulled back and smoothed out of her face, her red uniform jacket and immense kindness in her brown eyes. "I'd be impressed if anyone who grew up here couldn't tell you the story as they know it, but for the history I'd suggest the Willamette Valley History Museum." She rummaged behind her counter and manifested a white business card with simple, black writing. "Nathan LeBlanc. He's the curator but is very knowledgeable about local history, including the Woman in the River."

Beaming, Duncan took the card. "Wow. The history jackpot."

Nelson leaned in next to Duncan, but without actually touching the counter. "What do *you* know about the legend? Just out of curiosity." He held up the handheld camera. "For research purposes."

"Oh." She smoothed down the invisible stray hairs from her ponytail and smiled for the camera. "Well, like most people I've heard that she drowned her kids. Boys, I think. And now hunts the children of Portland at night. She specifically looks for bad kids who have disobeyed their mothers or whatever."

"And then what?" Nelson coaxed, his eye watching Marie through the camera lens.

"Then what, what?" Marie wrinkled her brow.

"What does she do to the children she takes? The ones who disobeyed?"

"Oh." Marie looked to the ceiling for the answers. "I never heard that part. Just that she hunts kids." She wagged a finger in mock scolding at Duncan and Nelson. "So, you'd better be good for goodness' sake."

And then she laughed at her own joke.

But Duncan and Nelson just stared.

Duncan turned to Nelson. "That's a very good question, Nelson. We need to find the story of someone who was taken."

"You don't..." Marie shook her head, the whites of her eyes plainly visible. "I mean, you don't actually think kids are being taken by a ghost, do you?"

"If you saw your son carried off by a woman as black as a shadow and then you chased them down to the river where your son was choking on water, what would you assume had happened?" Duncan asked her in response.

"Oh." Marie felt a chill wash over her. "I suppose I would think that was the Woman in the River. But..."

"That's what happened to our client." Duncan stood up tall, towering over both the desk and Marie. "Thanks for this." He held up the glossy white business card of Nathan LeBlanc.

Nelson held a hand up to wave goodbye. "Have a good day!"

Marie watched them leave, still processing the conversation.

Duncan drove his beat-up Chevy to the Willamette Valley History Museum. It was a short ten-minute drive along damp roads, but no rain was falling. Trees and greenery lined the streets the whole way there. The museum itself was a simple and unassuming building. It was gray, the same color as the stones that coated its exterior and the clouds that filled the sky, with a row of windows indicating a second story.

And it was quiet, with—eerily—no cars in the parking lot. Not even of the people who might work there.

With a slam of his car door, Duncan stated, "I wonder if Nathan LeBlanc is even here."

"I think so." Nelson pointed up at a light in one of the windows.

"I guess it's not the popular thing to do, learn about history on a Sunday morning."

Nelson shook his head. "Do people even care about history anymore?"

Duncan could only shrug. "Not about the Willamette Valley, I suppose."

The front door was unlocked, so they let themselves in. A small chime alerted whoever might be in the building that there were actually visitors here. It appeared empty, but the lit-up display cases and large graphics on the wall made it very clear that this was, in fact, the history museum they were looking for.

Nelson stood before a small glass case. "Look at this, Duncan."

"The Missoula Flood," Duncan read off the placard that sat outside the case.

"That's what makes it good for farming." Nelson pointed at the small diorama that visually told the story of how the flood from ten thousand years ago had defined the landscape and soil that the inhabitants enjoyed at present day.

"Lovers of history, welcome!" A man with slicked back hair and a blue blazer with patches on the elbows held his arms out wide as he announced his entrance to Duncan and Nelson.

"Would you be Nathan LeBlanc?" Duncan asked in response.

"I would indeed!" His smile never wavered and joy radiated off him. Whether it was from people finally coming to his museum or because he was excited that they knew who he was, Duncan couldn't be sure.

"Duncan. Paranormal Investigators League." Duncan stuck a hand out and watched the man's face fall before he shook the outstretched hand with little gusto. "We're told you know the history of the Woman in the River."

Nathan was offended. He didn't even try to hide it as he slicked back his hair, despite there being not a single hair out of place. He rivaled only Nelson in his put-together appearance. Duncan, on the other hand, looked a heartbeat away from living on the streets, with curly medium-length hair that fell whichever way it wanted and rarely saw the better part of a hairbrush.

"If you've come here to mock our local legends for your YouTube channel, you can just leave." Nathan gestured to the stairs he had just descended moments ago. "I have a very important project I am in the middle of."

"What kind of project?" Nelson asked sincerely. "I'm a scientist and it sometimes makes me very curious about the research of learned men such as yourself."

"Scientist?" Nathan asked Nelson but stared at Duncan, as if there were no possible way that these two could be here together. And both be part of such a ridiculous thing as a paranormal investigation.

"We're not here to mock you, Mr. LeBlanc." Duncan steepled his fingers together and spoke calmly. "We help people who are experiencing paranormal disturbances."

"We help the ghosts too," Nelson added with an adjustment of his black-rimmed glasses.

"Scientifically?" Nathan's disdain was evident.

Nelson shrugged. "Sometimes."

"Our client's son was taken by a woman who tried to drown him in the Tualatin River behind her house. She carried him down a steep drop-off which reduces the likelihood that he was taken by a mortal woman. So, one of the theories that has been presented is the Woman in the River." Duncan was still speaking slowly and calmly, as if to keep a scared cat from jumping.

"Young son?" Nathan asked.

Duncan nodded. "Nine."

Nathan let out a gush of air. And then turned to Nelson. "I'm working on a paper about the local trade habits of the indigenous people of the Willamette Valley. Before the white settlers and early pioneers. "

Nelson nodded. "That sounds amazing. I'd love to read it when you're done."

"Mr. LeBlanc, what do you know about the Woman in the River?" Duncan asked.

Nathan didn't answer right away. He turned and walked toward the room behind the entry way, gesturing for the investigators to follow. "This region really didn't become populated until the 1800's. Up until then, the local tribes enjoyed quite a bit of peace. When the pioneers began heading out west on the Oregon Trail, they brought many ethnic backgrounds. And a variety of languages."

"Looking for gold." Duncan nodded. He had learned the same history in his classes in California.

"Yes, mostly. Once the rumor of gold got around,

it did bring many an early settler with dreams of striking it rich," Nathan explained. "But there were some who came here for different reasons."

"Such as?"

"Some wanted to get rich taking advantage of the miners. Some needed freedom." Nathan pointed to a small sepia-colored image hung like a painting in the corner. "And some just hoped for a better life because they were so heavily persecuted back East. They figured it couldn't be worse."

"And this woman was one of them?" Duncan pointed at the picture hanging on the wall.

"Marchesa Carolina De Ragnoni," Nathan stated with a thick Italian accent and a flourish of his hand. "An Italian noblewoman with two young sons in tow. Or so she told everyone. She came out west with no husband and no given reason as to why she was traveling alone. Highly unusual for a woman—especially a mother—at that time."

"What did she do once she got here?" Duncan asked.

"She set up a business as a laundress. Mining was really dirty work and there was no indoor plumbing so... Let's just say she was busy. And able to build a decent life for her two sons."

"Any clue what the young sons were named?" Nelson asked.

Nathan shook his head. "Lost to history, I'm sorry to say." He lowered his voice and leaned in, as if speaking of such things might offend the picture on the wall. "They both died before maturity."

"So, this is the Woman in the River? This Marchesa?" Duncan asked, pointing directly at her sepia image. Her hair was pulled back in the image and her expression was sour. Small curls accented her face.

"Yes.   This   Marchesa-turned-laundress murdered her two young sons by drowning them in the Willamette." Nathan frowned at the horrible tale, but more for dramatic effect than heartfelt pity.

"And what happened to the Marchesa?" Nelson asked.

Nathan held up a finger.   "This is where

historical facts get murky. The short answer: she also died. That much we know is true. Shortly after she killed her sons, she was also found floating in the river face down. *But.*"

Dramatic pause. And Duncan took the bait. "Yes?"

"The rumors swirled around about how she died and, it being the mid-nineteenth century, no forensic analysis was ever done. She drowned. Case closed. Another murderer off the streets."

"But what on earth would make her kill her sons in the first place?" Nelson asked.

"Aah. Now you're getting to the heart of the matter!" Nathan aimed his pointer finger at Nelson for emphasis. "And again, historically speaking, we don't know."

"How about the rumors? We'll take those," Duncan said.

Nelson joined Duncan's questioning. "Those are often quite helpful for us, to be honest."

"They run the gamut, of course." With each

theory he rattled off, Nathan gestured with his hands. "She was possessed. She snapped one day and went crazy. Her sons were the real murderers, so she had to kill them, as if their murder was somehow noble."

"I'm sensing there's a 'but' in there?" Duncan asked.

"Well, there was one theory that seemed to gain the most traction. The one that most people believed. It even ran in the papers at the time as if it were fact, but it wasn't. Rumors only." Nathan shook his head. "Journalistic integrity was different at that time."

Duncan prodded. "What was the prevailing theory?"

"That Italian hit men were sent to find her and her sons, killing them before they told whatever secret they knew. Mobsters, essentially." Nathan laughed to himself. "Even back then people loved a good conspiracy that points at the Italian Mob."

But Duncan and Nelson weren't laughing. They exchanged a look.

"So she really might have been a victim," Duncan

said, voicing his thoughts.

"One other thing that's bothering me," Nelson said. "If she went out west, which was a very hard trip, with nothing but her sons and the clothes on her back, and then worked hard to set up her business to make a better life for her children, why would she kill them?"

"Maybe the mob got them first," Duncan proposed. "Kids do make easier prey."

"You're not..." Nathan scoffed, an almost-gurgling sound rumbling in his throat, giving a noise to indicate the word 'preposterous.' "You're not actually running with the mob idea, are you?"

"It seems to fit, don't you think?" Duncan asked.

Nathan shook his head. "No. She was just a woman who went crazy and killed her sons and then herself."

"That's certainly a possibility too," Duncan acknowledged.

"But it doesn't fit the circumstantial evidence. Circumstantially she was escaping something and then thriving in this new community." Nelson looked from

Nathan to Duncan, daring each to argue with him. "And then something happened." Nelson snapped his fingers. "And they're all dead."

"I agree," Duncan said, nodding. "She went crazy is a convenient excuse. Possible, but a little too easy."

"So, you both are telling me that the woman whose ghost wanders around taking other people's children for all eternity like a boogeyman was somehow victimized?" Nathan couldn't even hide his disgust with such a ridiculous notion. "Then why on earth would people still be afraid of her? If she was so victimized?"

Duncan pointed at Nathan, as if he were part of their theorizing squad and not the naysayer he was trying to be. "Yes. Exactly."

Nathan waited impatiently for more explanation from Duncan.

But it was Nelson who began expanding on the theory pool. "Well, we'll have to get the answer to that, of course, but it could be that she's cursed to do so. It could also be that she is just confused and truly looking for her sons and then grabs the boys who look similar. Or perhaps she is simply misguided, thinking that this is her only chance at retribution."

"And how, exactly, do you suppose you're going to get answers, as you say?" Nathan literally looked down his nose at Nelson, the whole conversation having left the land of sanity some minutes ago.

"We'll probably have to ask her."

"Yeah, no doubt we're going to need to talk to her at some point," Duncan added. He turned to Nathan. "Which is where we'll need your help. Do you know exactly where she died?"

Despite the deep crease in his forehead that announced his skepticism, Nathan answered the question. "No. We only know where she was found. Along the banks of the Willamette River."

"That'll work." Duncan clapped his hands together, ready to get to work.

"Can you point out the location on a map? So we know where to conduct our next investigation?" Nelson asked.

"Well, yeah." Nathan looked like a man who had lost his place in this conversation, but was finally getting to something he actually could participate in. "Let me show you."

Nathan led the investigators back to the room they had been standing in originally. On a far back wall was a large aerial image of the Willamette River, small labels marking points of interest all along the way.

"It's behind a grocery store today, but it was just a muddy bank back in the eighteen hundreds, of course." Nathan pointed at the river with his finger, indicating a blank space between Elk Rock Garden and Dunthorpe.

"Oh, Duncan. You should take a picture," Nelson suggested.

"Oh, yeah." As Duncan dug around in his pockets looking for his phone, he asked Nelson, "Where's your phone?"

Nelson shrugged. "No idea."

Duncan took the picture of the area where the Woman in the River, the Marchesa de Ragnoni, was eventually found drowned under mysterious circumstances.

And a good next place to try to find her.

"Thank you, Mr. LeBlanc. You've been very helpful," Duncan said as he put his phone away.

"Yes," Nelson added. "Where they died is often a large connection to their phantasmic energy."

"We'll let you know what she tells us, so you can perfect those theories," Duncan added, as if Nathan even wanted to know.

"Oh, absolutely. This will make potentially your greatest book!" Nelson beamed.

Nathan, on the other hand, continued to curl his lip, relaxing only once the investigators had gone and he could resume his solitary work in the real world.

He couldn't remember a conversation so ridiculous in his entire academic life.

Chapter 6 – All We Know So Far

The clock was just about to strike four in the afternoon, the hour when they had all agreed to meet back up in the hotel lobby coffee shop. The sun squeezed just a sliver of light between two clouds, pushing its way through enough to allow the skinniest ray of sunshine down upon the Tualatin. Duncan stared at that tiny sliver of light that had persevered where so many other rays had given up in their confrontation.

All around that sun ray were blankets and blankets of gray clouds.

"Looks like it may rain again," Nelson stated the obvious.

Duncan lifted his foot, dangling his flip-flop from between two toes. "I guess I should probably change shoes before we investigate tonight."

Nelson nodded. "Paige will likely yell at you if you don't anyway."

The thud of the laptop on the table announced Duane's presence. "Caught two things. But mostly it was quiet."

"The shadow? In the forest?" Duncan asked.

But Duane shook his head. "That was just the form the shadow took in the moonlight. It was nothing."

"Huh." Duncan scratched his cheek as he mulled over his mistaken intuition.

"The Woman in the River was an Italian Marchesa," Nelson explained, eager to share what they had learned.

Duane sat in the chair opposite Nelson. "Is that supposed to impress me?"

Nelson shrugged. "I thought it was interesting."

Duncan leaned back. "She may not have killed herself. It might have been murder. Let's see what Paige uncovered."

As if they had planned it, Paige waltzed in the glass double doors, beaming. "She's an Italian Marchesa!"

"Why is everyone so excited about that? Rich

Italians die too, you know?" Duane asked the team.

"That's like Duchess or Countess, Duane. She wasn't just rich. She was rich *and powerful.* And then somehow she ended up penniless in Oregon. It's such an amazing testament to the Oregon Trail." Paige sighed as she found the seat opposite Duncan. "People from all walks of life heading out west to seek fame and fortune."

Duane shook his head. "No. People don't risk everything they have, including their lives, if their lives are amazing. And they're rich and powerful with Italian titles. I don't buy it."

Duncan snapped his fingers. "I agree. Running from someone or something because you're scared does make more sense than a romantic dream of living out west."

Paige frowned. "I didn't find anything that said she was running from someone."

"The historian at the museum Nelson and I visited said one of the rumors was the mob got her."

Even Paige was skeptical. "The mob? Really? It doesn't get more cliché."

"You guys are forgetting the number one thing we all should have learned by now," Duane said, raising an eyebrow. "People who curse and get cursed are liars." He leaned back in his chair. "She wasn't an Italian Marchesa. You come out west, you change your name and give yourself a title and a new backstory and hide in plain sight. I'll bet the real Marchesa died under mysterious circumstances and cursed her murderer."

Nelson, Paige and Duncan were silent while they digested all that Duane had said—which were more words than he usually spoke.

Nelson was the first to speak. "Fair point, Duane. That is actually a theory with a high likelihood of possibility."

"What did you find out, Paige?" Duncan asked.

Paige shrugged. "Doesn't sound like much more than you. Except. I did find one article from New York that sounded like evidence to me that she was who she said she was." Paige dug around in her oversized bag and pulled out some printed pages. She slapped them on the table they were sitting around, but the loose papers fell with more of a gentle rustle.

"What does it say?" Duncan asked.

Duane rolled his eyes. "Paige. After all these years, you should know no one is going to read your printouts."

"But we're very interested in what you learned." Nelson did not deny what Duane stated, Paige noticed.

"Fine." Paige scooped back up her papers. "The article was about the death of her husband in New York before she decided to come out west. It calls him Marchese Luigi De Ragnoni. He left behind a wife, Carolina. So at least as far back as New York her title seems to be true."

"Does it mention cause of death?" Duane asked.

"No, just says he died peacefully," Paige explained.

"Does it talk about their two sons?" Nelson asked.

Paige frowned. "No, now that you mention it."

"Let me see those." Nelson reached across the table to grab the printouts from Paige's hands, which she gave willingly. At last, someone else wanted to read her pages. "The Marchese is survived by his wife, Marchesa Carolina De Ragnoni," Nelson read. He let go of the papers and let them float gently back to the tabletop. "No mention of their sons."

"Interesting." Duncan ran his fingers through his long bangs, pulling them back out of his face. "So her husband dies and she has no sons. She shows up out west with two boys she claims are her sons."

"It is possible the newspaper just didn't mention the children, ya know," Paige said.

"Possible, but unlikely. It's pretty standard to list out everyone you are survived by, especially in the case of someone with a title and nobility. Young sons would mean carrying on the lineage," Nelson explained.

"Which is probably exactly why she kidnapped two random boys to make them be her sons," Duane snorted. "If the titles need a male to pass on to, she also loses everything when her husband dies."

"Maybe they're adopted? It could have been done legally," Paige argued.

"Did you find any paperwork to support it, Paige?" Duncan asked her.

"Well, no."

"That doesn't necessarily mean anything," Nelson explained. "Nothing was digital back then, so papers got lost, burnt in fires, destroyed all the time. If they were even kept in the first place, which wasn't a given."

"So, she is living her best life in New York with her rich Marchese husband and no children. He dies and then she appears in Oregon with two sons. And then not much after that, she and her boys also end up dead. How much time had passed between her husband's death and when she appears in Oregon?" Duncan asked.

Paige lifted the papers to read the date. "He died October ninth, eighteen fifty-two."

"And the Marchesa died in eighteen fifty-four," Nelson explained.

Duncan let out a long, slow whistle. "Very tight timeframe we're working with."

"So, the mystery is where those two boys came

from?" Paige proposed.

"And why they all ended up dead," Duncan added.

Duane grunted, slouching in his seat. "The real question is who this lady was *really*, cuz I'm willing to bet she wasn't *the* Carolina De Ragnoni. The real Marchesa died along with her husband and this chick was committing identity fraud."

"Was there anything in your research about why the Marchese came to New York in the first place?" Duncan asked Paige. "I agree with Duane that people don't typically leave their homeland and everything they know because things are going well."

Paige tightened her mouth for a moment and then lunged for the papers so fast that Duane leaned away from her energy. "I think I do remember something about that." With a buoyancy only Paige could muster, she scanned the pages from the obituary and then dug in her bag for more when the original papers failed to answer the question. "Here. This might be a clue."

She pointed at a sentence on one of the pages she held close to Duncan's face. To oblige her, he read aloud for the team. "The Marchese De Ragnoni was an asylum seeker after his failed coup during the political unrest of the 1840's. His decision to defy his own noble birth and take to arms with the Nationalist group known as 'Young Italy' would set the course for the rest of his life."

"So he was a revolutionary? That would give plenty of reasons for someone to want to kill him." Nelson nodded as he spoke.

"Too easy," Duane answered.

But Paige turned in her seat, arm resting on the back of her chair, to challenge Duane. "If she's an identity thief, I agree with you. But if she is who she says she is, then the simplest answer could be the right one."

Nelson adjusted his black-rimmed glasses. "He has to run for his life from the Italian government he stood up against. They chase him to New York and execute him for his high crimes. Then his wife heads west, presumably scared for her own life, and then appears as a laundress in Oregon with two kids in tow." Nelson paused in thought for a moment. "Yeah, the kids for sure are the wildcard. She clearly wasn't trying to be a Marchesa anymore, or why would she head to Oregon where no one would care?"

"So, for sure, there's at least one group of people who would want the Marchese dead. And did his wife want that also?" Paige leaned across the table to Nelson. "But what if there was something in New York he also got himself mixed up in and *those* people wanted him dead too?"

Nelson half-whispered. "Maybe it was the mob, after all."

"Well, we can theorize until the cows come home, but we need to get real answers. Paige, can you call the Mellins and tell them we have nothing yet to show them?" Duncan asked.

"You got it!" Paige practically jumped out of her seat with determination. Duane watched her bounce to the entrance of the hotel with an eyebrow raised.

"I suppose there's a séance in our future?"

Nelson asked.

Duncan nodded. "I think we all know there is only one way to get to the bottom of this."

Duane and Nelson answered in unison. "Talk to the ghost."

Duncan clapped his hands together. "Let's gear up. We're going to the Willamette River to do some Marchesa-ghost-hunting."

Chapter 7 – The Muddy Banks

"Do we trust this ghost?" Duane asked Duncan as they worked to set up their cameras away from the muddy river's edge. The tripod was angled on the hill and Duane worked to countersink one of the legs into the grass.

"Do we have a choice?" Duncan asked back.

"I think so." Duane rubbed his forehead to wipe away the moisture that had accumulated from the drizzle in the air. "I think I may have an idea."

"Really, Duncan?" Paige walked by with the black duffle bag that carried their spices and candles. "It's going to start raining soon."

Duncan lifted a foot to double-check his footwear and then let the flip-flop land back on the ground with a loud snap. "I forgot to change my shoes."

"I'll say." Paige shook her head. "Don't blame me if you get pneumonia."

Ignoring Paige, Duane continued their earlier conversation. "I think we should call the Marchese. The husband. Instead of the Woman in the River. Ask him what actually happened."

"Or even the kids," Nelson added, walking up from the river. "Paige is good with kids. And we've had decent results with the ghosts of children in other cases."

"Not that close to the water, Paige!" Duane shouted down the hill and then groaned. "I'll do it."

Nelson looked to Duncan, who shrugged. "He likes to do it."

Duane ran down to the river and grabbed the bag from Paige. Nelson and Duncan watched as Duane carefully moved each of the candles Paige had already set up back from the water by about ten feet. It wasn't an ocean current or anything, so Duncan suspected they didn't need to expect a big wave, but he also was willing to admit that none of them knew much about the current patterns of rivers. There weren't any rivers running near Hollywood and Vine in Los Angeles.

"I say we call them all and see who shows up," Duncan announced to his team.

Nelson scrunched his lips as he debated Duncan's idea and then nodded. "I can go along with that. Expect the unexpected, as they say."

"Fine." Duane stood, arms folded across his chest. "But if only *she* shows up, we fact-check her later."

Paige nodded. "I agree. And I'd be happy to research anything she tells us."

"Are we good to go dark?" Duncan asked Duane.

Duane looked up at the sky where the sun hadn't begun to set, but the clouds made it appear closer to sunset. "Candles are set up, if that's what you mean."

"Places for the séance," Duncan instructed, calling back over his shoulder to Nelson.

As Nelson joined the team near the river where the candles were set up, Duncan grabbed Paige's hand. They stood in a small circle, holding hands. The misty drizzle swirled around them giving their work a gothic vibe.

Paige, Nelson and Duane started humming while Duncan called to the spirits of the deceased, reciting the words he had done so many times as to know them by heart. Ever since he'd been introduced to the power of the séance by Daphne all those years ago, Duncan had understood that the spirit world was something to be respected, not feared. And what drove the fear was the ignorance. And the only path out of ignorance was to ask questions.

And so, séance.

"There's something in the middle of the water," Nelson announced to the team.

Paige turned to look over her shoulder but really couldn't see much in the misty air. "What do you see, Nelson?"

"It's like a heavier mist in the middle of the river. Maybe like a human form. Keep going, Duncan." Nelson kept his eye strained in the direction of the heavy mist. It was too soon to know if it was a ghost, or simply heavy mist in an area of the country where heavy mist was standard fare.

Duncan kept repeating the incantation as the team strained their eyes to see something—anything—out on the water.

"Who calls me?"

When Paige heard the voice over her shoulder, she screamed. In the middle of their circle a woman with a long black veil had appeared. While they had all been staring out at the river.

"That was a jump scare," Paige explained her scream.

"I really thought I saw a figure on the water. Sorry," Nelson answered.

"Who are you?" Duane stuck out his chin as he asked the first question.

"La Marchesa," the figure answered in a heavy Italian accent. Certainly, whoever the ghost was, she wasn't faking her Italian language skills.

"Why do you terrorize young children in this community?" Duncan asked.

"Why do *they* terrorize me?" the Marchesa asked back.

"I know the boys you drowned weren't really yours," Paige announced, no real question forming.

"I drown no one. Lies," she hissed back.

"We want to help you, but to do that we need to understand," Duncan explained.

The ghost whipped her head around to Duncan so fast there was a blur of black veil. "You can't understand. And you can't help me." Her defiance softened. "No one can."

"We've helped many ghosts, just like you. But first we have to know what happened to you," Duncan explained. "Were you cursed?"

"Murdered?" Nelson asked.

"Betrayed?" Paige.

"Avenged?" Duane.

"A kidnapper?" Paige added.

"Or a murderer yourself?" Duane asked.

Duncan couldn't remember hearing a ghost sigh before, but the Woman in the River before him sure sounded like she did.

"You can't understand."

"Noooooooo!" The cry came from the middle of the river and grew louder as it flew toward them. A figure floated toward them and disappeared when it got close.

And then both the figure from the water and the woman in the center of the séance were gone.

"I knew I'd seen something on the river," Nelson beamed.

"That's the guy we needed. The Marchese." Duane flopped his arms at his side.

"We don't know that that was the Marchese. Could have been one of the many victims she's left in her wake." Duncan peered out at the water, hoping the second ghost would reappear.

"They were mad that she was talking to us," Nelson said. "That's a contextual clue. Why would the Marchese not want her speaking to us?"

"Because. She's a liar." Duane rolled his eyes.

"Actually, when people silence others it tends to be because they are telling the truth." Paige's words filled the air all around them, swirling in the mist and clumping like the moisture that collected in their hair and clothing. No one argued.

"Back to the mob theory." Nelson nodded as he spoke.

"Back where we started. She told us nothing." Duncan frowned as he kicked a rock.

"She did say one thing kind of interesting," Paige offered. "She said the locals were terrorizing her."

"If she *is* telling the truth, I could see where she'd be frustrated." Nelson used his fingers to punctuate each event on the timeline. "First, they had to escape the country of their birth. Never an easy thing to do. Next, her husband dies and she needs to flee her new adopted city." Nelson looked at Duane. "Yes, perhaps it's because she was fleeing the scene of the crime. I'll grant you that. And finally, she comes out west to start anew and then she gets harassed again." He shook his head. Not a single hair budged with the movement. "If those are the high points, it's pretty depressing."

"So what do we do now?" Paige asked the group,

although her eyes were focused on Duncan.

Duncan shrugged. "I think we pack it up for tonight. I'd like to watch the footage and see if we can identify the ghost that chased off the Marchesa. And maybe, just maybe, we can learn something new from this experience."

Nelson put a hand on Duncan's shoulder. "You know how ghost-hunting goes. You get what you get. And you don't throw a fit."

Duncan wrinkled his brow. "I've never said that before."

Instead of answering, Nelson just shrugged.

Assuming the time for conversation was over, Duane dropped to his knees and began packing up the séance by the river. The fog was getting thicker anyway, making it harder and harder to see anything. The moisture in the air would've extinguished their candles sooner or later.

Paige wrapped her arms around herself, fighting off a sudden chill. They'd worked in colder places than this, but in the fog by the river, somehow

Portland was feeling surprisingly crisp.

Duncan turned to walk up the hill where the camera had been filming the séance on the tripod, but he'd only gotten a few steps when he reacted.

"Ow! Who did that?" Duncan turned back to the team, rubbing the back of his head.

Nelson, Paige and Duane all stared at one another, each waiting for the other to speak. But certainly, no one had seen anyone do anything.

"Who did what, Duncan?" Paige asked.

"Never mind. I see." With a nod of his head, he gestured behind Paige's shoulder.

Paige slow-turned to look behind herself, the air getting even colder as she did. Her bottom lip shook as it turned blue, the air feeling as if they'd passed through some sort of a portal into a walk-in freezer.

Despite her shivers, though, she knew what Duncan was referring to the instant she turned. There, hidden in the fog, was the form of a young boy. He seemed to be solid, and yet not, almost as if he himself was made from the moisture in the air. But if that wasn't enough to tell Paige they were talking to the ghost of a child, his old-style clothing certainly was.

"Do you have something to tell us, little one?" Paige asked, doing her best to sound like a trustworthy teacher.

But the little boy never opened his mouth.

He pointed a cold, blue finger to the ground directly beneath his feet. And then the fog twisted and turned until there was nothing left to see but white mist. The ghost boy had vanished.

Paige exchanged a look with Duncan.

"What was all that about?" Duncan asked.

Paige frowned. "I have no idea."

"He was clearly trying to tell us something," Nelson answered. "He pointed at the ground. Why?"

"And he didn't speak. He was probably scared of whoever was on the water." Paige folded her arms. "We've seen this before, Duncan. The other ghost is the aggressor."

"Maybe. Maybe not. But it still doesn't make any sense." Duncan scratched his cheek. "Why does the

Woman in the River still hunt children? And what do these other ghosts have to do with anything? Absolutely nothing is fitting together."

"We have to watch more footage and do more research. Clearly." Duane stood up and tossed the duffel bag over one shoulder. And then he marched up the hill.

Duncan didn't argue. Turning on his heel, he finished what he'd started and took down the camera and tripod on the hill.

"I guess we're done here." Nelson removed his glasses and wiped the gathered condensation on his shirt.

"Good. I'm freezing." Without waiting for Nelson, Paige stormed up the hill after Duane.

Chapter 8 – Who's The Guy?

Duane was thankful that they hadn't had too late of a night ghost-hunting. He got a good night's sleep—a rarity—and he was now able to focus his energy on watching the footage from the river. He might even have the energy to re-watch the footage from the first night behind the Mellins' property.

Duncan was always saying to trust your instincts, and Duane's instincts said there was something he didn't like about the Marchesa being an innocent victim who went around murdering children.

It didn't add up.

In the darkness of his hotel room, he placed the headphones over his ears, the headband resting cold and hard on his bald head.

Duncan had already left for the day, off to research with Nelson and Paige. That was fine for Duane. He preferred doing this work himself.

And alone.

People like Duncan and Paige always felt a need to fill the silence with their talking.

He pressed play on the footage and watched the scenic view go crooked and then straight again as Duncan adjusted and repositioned the camera. He heard his own voice as he chastised Paige for not setting up the ceremony correctly, shaking his head at the memory. Hearing or seeing himself on camera always made him uncomfortable.

Despite a strong desire to skip ahead to when the Marchesa first appeared, Duane remained steadfast on watching every single moment they'd captured. Whether he believed there might be anything to see or not was immaterial. This was his job. His responsibility. To ensure that the team didn't miss a single clue they'd captured, even if they didn't realize what they had at the time.

And that was common. Duane often captured shadows, swirls, footsteps and even voices. It was rarer still, but sometimes he was able to see full body apparitions that they had been completely ignorant of during the investigation.

The time ticked on and his instincts proved to be right. It was just the four PIL members talking, setting up, chanting.

And then the Marchesa appeared in the center of the circle. But that's not what Duane focused on. He had seen her there that night, and so was unimpressed that she appeared on the footage. What was much more interesting to him was the figure Nelson had claimed to see in the middle of the river.

The swirl of mist was visible on the video they'd captured. Too nebulous to offer any clue to what figure it formed but solidified enough that Duane felt confident he was seeing a ghost. Yes, he wanted to prove it was the Marchese himself, but Duane was a good enough investigator to remain impartial and watch where the clues led him.

He made a note in his notebook of the time stamp and continued watching.

He watched as they interacted with the

Marchesa. Nothing new to see there. She protested innocence, and Duane rolled his eyes as he watched.

But then, the misty form on the river took on shape and hurled toward the Marchesa. Duane sat up straight and paused the footage, just a second too late to see anything on the frozen frame but a swirl of movement. But Duane was a seasoned professional. He knew exactly how to walk the footage back frame by frame until he could see what he needed to see.

"Well, I'll be..." Duane murmured to himself as he jotted down the time stamp, eyes glued to the image before him.

There were most definitely *two* ghosts in this frozen frame. With the ghost child Paige saw later in the night, that made three. And could there be another little boy?

Fighting the urge to jump to conclusions, Duane hit the call button on Duncan's name.

"Talk to me, Duane." Duncan's voice came through loud and clear on his cell phone.

"Duncan, I can see the swirly mist Nelson

flagged on the river. I'll grab a screenshot for you. He's misty, but it's definitely the outline of a man." Duane spoke in crisp words, matter of fact. He might be short-tempered at times, and glass-half-empty almost always, but he was a hell of an investigator. He knew that about himself. And so he knew this was a hell of a clue.

"Well, all right. Now we're finally getting somewhere," Duncan responded. Duane could see his lead investigator bouncing on his feet. There were few six-and-a-half foot men that bounced like a child, but that was Duncan.

"We need to find out who this guy is. Of course, my mind went to the Marchese, but it could be anybody. Even someone who lived here in Oregon at the time she died." Duane stated the obvious.

"Agreed. Send me the pic and Paige and I will dig through the archives to see if we can identify him."

"And Nelson?" Duane grunted.

"Documenting EMF readings along the Tualatin and Willamette Rivers," Duncan explained.

"Uh." Half uh-huh and half grunt was Duane's

response.

After hanging up with Duncan, Duane remembered that they had had another encounter right before they left. Paige had seen the little boy, presumably one of the drowned sons of the Marchesa.

As he continued scrutinizing the video for further evidence, Duane thought about what kind of person would drown their sons. And then he remembered that these might not be her children. And then it dawned on him that perhaps lies were obfuscating the truth.

What if the Marchesa was telling a kernel of truth amongst her lies?

It angered him to accept that reality, but he knew well after all the cases across the country they had worked that a liar could sometimes tell the truth. And a mostly honest person could sometimes lie.

And then he stood straight up in his chair. They hadn't seen it that night, or at least not realized it, but the little boy was not alone.

"Who the hell is that guy?"

Chapter 9 – Twists and Turns

"Duncan, we have had to do some very bizarre things in our line of work. But matching a swirling mist to actual photographs? That might take the cake." Paige shook her head as she rifled through the article she'd printed previously, hunting for the photograph of the Marchese.

"The Marchesa is kidnapping children in the night and taking them down to the river. That much we know is true." Duncan held his phone up for Paige to see the misty form. "But what is actually going on? Feels like we got nothing."

"I believe the Marchesa. I think she's a victim." Paige frowned as she spoke. When at last she'd found the photo she was looking for, she held it up next to Duncan's phone. "Not him."

Duncan squinted and leaned in. "How can you

tell?"

"Right there." She pointed at the sepia-colored picture on her printout. "The Marchese's forehead is much smaller. Clean haircut. Mustache. Long story short, the Marchese looks rich. This misty formed guy looks like a thug."

Duncan stood up straight and folded his arms. "Excuse me, but disheveled doesn't necessarily mean thug."

"I didn't mean to insult all people less concerned with their looks." Paige placed an apologetic hand on Duncan's arm, carefully ignoring a glance at his baggy, wrinkled clothes. "I meant that the swirly guy doesn't present himself as royalty."

"Okay. So, someone other than the Marchese was there at the river last night and angry that the Marchesa was talking." Duncan scratched his chin. "But who the heck is this guy?"

"We'll be grasping at straws unless we have some kind of clue who it could be." Paige tucked the printout back in her oversized shoulder bag.

Duncan snapped at Paige. "We know she was a local laundress. Maybe we start with locals who could have been her customers."

Paige frowned. "Duncan, that could be anyone."

"This was the frontier. Towns were not exactly filled with half a million people yet."

"So what are you proposing?" Paige asked, looking up at her boss.

"We're looking between 1852 and 1854. We can start with local newspapers from that time period and see what we find." Duncan started marching to the periodicals, but Paige grabbed his arm to stop him.

"But this guy could have followed them from Italy. We don't know that he was a local. We know her story ended here, but it didn't begin here," Paige explained.

"Good point." Duncan pointed at Paige. "You look for known associates in Italy and I'll look for known associates in Oregon. And between us, I hope we find the swirly dude."

The hours at the local library were long and, for

Duncan, very boring. Paige loved researching and digging into history. Duncan found it torturous.

And the question still remained. Was the Marchesa the perpetrator or the victim? Or even both? And once they knew, what would they do about it?

What felt like an eternity later, Paige and Duncan regrouped at the table they were working on in the middle of the library. Since it was the middle of the day in the middle of the week, the place was quiet and mostly empty. An occasional mom might have a young child in tow near the children's section, or a college-aged student might be quietly studying in a corner, but by and large Paige and Duncan felt they had the library to themselves.

"Whatcha got?" Duncan asked as he flopped into his seat.

"Well. I'm not sure it's anything." True to her form, Paige whipped out a stack of printouts.

Duncan whistled. "You always find so much stuff."

"Let's compare our findings to your swirly mist."

Paige leaned in and held up each printout, one by one, to the image of the mist. On maybe the fifth or sixth printout, Paige asked, "What about this one?"

Duncan leaned in and squinted. "A definite maybe. He for sure captures the thug vibe."

Paige shoved Duncan playfully. "Okay. I'll put that one aside."

"Who was he?"

"Uh…" Paige re-read the printout to double-check. "Co-founder of the Young Italy and best friends with the Marchese de Ragnoni."

"Best friend in love with the wife tryst?" Duncan raised an eyebrow.

"No clue." Paige shrugged.

"Well, here's who I found. The most thuggy of them all was this guy. Karl Van Mussen. He was like a local crime-lord-mob-boss sort of guy. Ran all the seedy businesses and made a fortune doing it. Loved to show off his money so no doubt needed to look sharp."

"And therefore would likely outsource his laundry?" Paige asked.

Duncan lifted his hands up to say 'who knows.' "It's true I might have focused more on character than any other trait." He held up his phone with the mist image. "What do we think?"

It was Paige's turn to scrutinize the comparison. "Hmmm. The same big forehead and unruly curls." She leaned back. "Possible."

"Add this to the 'maybe' pile then if you would please." Duncan handed his printout to Paige and she piled it on top of the best friend.

"Any others?" Duncan asked Paige.

"Yeah. Let's keep going." Paige held up another dozen images, one by one. None seemed quite as likely as the first two, but perhaps they were just going cross-eyed at the non-stop scrutinizing. They did manage to get another couple printouts in the 'maybe' pile. "What do you think our next move is?"

"I think we need to do more investigating at the river. We need to understand who the misty ghost is and what their relation is to the Marchesa, if they had anything to do with her death," Duncan answered.

"And the little boy ghost?" Paige asked.

Duncan shrugged. "He certainly could also have clues. I mean, she swears she never killed anyone and surely the little boy would know if she killed him."

"And if he's even her actual son. I'm curious to know more about that," Paige added as she shoved the printouts from the 'maybe' pile into her oversized bag.

"Yeah. This case has so many potential roads to nowhere." Duncan held his phone up as it buzzed in his hand. "Duane," he announced to Paige before he answered. "What's up, Duane?"

A few nods and uh-huhs later and the call was ended.

"What was all that about?" Paige asked, standing as she did and lifting her bag over her shoulder.

"He found something on the footage that he wants to share with the Mellins." Duncan began walking to the front of the library, weaving through stacks of books on his way from the tables to the front door.

Paige followed a few steps behind, especially since it took three of her steps to equal one of Duncan's.

"Are we heading back to the hotel?"

"No." Duncan kept walking with only a mere nod of his head toward Paige as he spoke. "We're meeting at their house."

"Don't you want to see the footage first?" Paige was shocked that they would watch the footage alongside the Mellin family. That never happened. And, depending on the family, sometimes they never showed the footage at all.

"I'm trusting Duane on this one," was all Duncan said in reply.

Paige knew Duane had many redeemable qualities. Despite his monosyllabic responses and often sour mood, he was a fantastic investigator with an incredible eye for detail. She knew if he'd found something in the footage that there was something substantial to share.

It was Duncan that was striking her as acting unusual. But she didn't push it. They chit-chatted on the way to the Mellin house, parking in front right behind the P.I.L. van.

Duane wasted no time in pulling up his laptop.

"Should we wait for Nelson?" Paige asked as she climbed out of Duncan's old Chevy.

"We can show him later," Duane replied, not waiting for anyone to agree. He opened his laptop and turned the screen toward them, then pressed play.

A few seconds rolled, they saw the figure behind the little boy, and it took a moment for them to process what Duane had found.

"Oh, wow," was Paige's response.

"I see now why you want to show this to the client, Duane," Duncan responded, rubbing his chin.

"Are we sure it's not the Marchesa?" Paige had to ask.

"No, I'm not sure. But this manifestation is different," Duane explained.

"And if she shows up every time she materializes, we'd need to understand why," Duncan added.

"Oh, there's Nelson." He climbed out of the rideshare and straightened his pants and glasses before joining his team. "Did you learn anything, Nelson?"

Nelson shook his head. "Readings are normal and consistent everywhere we investigated."

"Check out what Duane found." Duncan aimed a thumb at his bald investigator. After the clip rolled, it was Nelson's turn to rub his chin.

"Are we sure it's not the Marchesa?" Nelson asked.

"That's what I said!" Paige flopped her arms to accentuate the like-mindedness.

"Since we're already here, let's show the client. Get confirmation if this is who might have taken their child," Duncan said. "But we really do need answers. If this isn't the Marchesa, we need to know exactly who it is."

Leading the team toward the front of the house, Duncan knocked on the door. Lucy answered the door. Lines deepened across her forehead in ways that Duncan knew meant she had been very stressed out by her recent encounter with the supernatural. It was all too common.

"I'm realizing now that perhaps we should have called first, but we wanted to show you some of the footage we captured during our investigation," Duncan explained. "May we come in?"

After a moment of frozen shock, Lucy stepped aside saying, "Yes, of course."

As she led them back to the family room, she asked, "You have video evidence? Of a ghost?"

"A couple of ghosts, actually," Nelson blurted before realizing that perhaps he should learn to sugarcoat things like Duncan and Paige.

"A *couple* of ghosts? Meaning more than the one?" Lucy asked, complete astonishment covering her face.

At Paige's pointed look, Nelson had the decency to cower.

But Duncan didn't miss a beat. "It happens sometimes. Doesn't mean everything is related. But we talked to the Marchesa di Rignoni, the woman that history claims is the Woman in the River. And we have that evidence on video."

Duncan nodded to Duane, and he played the clip from the séance.

Lucy only stared, wide-eyed.

"But there was another woman in black there that night. One we hadn't noticed at the time." Again Duncan gave the signal to Duane. This time the clip was the entity standing behind the small child. A woman, all in black with her face covered with a black veil, stood menacingly behind the child.

Lucy gasped and covered her mouth.

"Could this be who you saw take your son?" Duncan dared to ask.

Lucy nodded, her eyes welling up with tears, the trauma from that awful experience coming back to her with the image on Duane's laptop. "Yes. I don't know anything about that Marchesa lady. But this is definitely the one who kidnapped and tried to kill my son."

Chapter 10 - The Woman in Black

"So, what are we thinking?" Duncan asked his team as they sat a few minutes later in the hotel lobby. A soft drizzle of rain had begun outside, making everything darker and creating rivulets of rain on the windows.

Paige shook her head. "It's not the Marchesa. No way. She was telling the truth all along."

"It could be the Marchesa," Nelson argued. "It is possible for an entity to appear in multiple ways. They don't always have to manifest the same way every time. Take Gunther's research on the Edinburgh Castle. He cited three ghosts manifesting such that it seemed there were twenty ghosts haunting the place. One ghost, multiple forms."

"Both things are possibilities," Duncan agreed. "But we need answers."

"This is going to surprise people." Duane folded

his arms and remained slouched with his hoodie up. He looked bored to be there. "But after watching this footage over and over, I'm with Paige. The scary lady in black doesn't vibe the same as the Marchesa. It's possible the Marchesa was a victim."

"That's very big of you, Duane." Paige placed a gentle hand on his arm and he grunted in response.

"So maybe she was truly on the run when she came out west?" Duncan asked.

"Maybe," Paige responded.

"Let's show them the contenders for the swirly mist," Duncan said to Paige, who pulled out the printouts from her bag.

"If it was someone from Italy, then we're thinking it's this guy, Antonio Luciano and the Marchese's best friend." Paige flipped to the printout Duncan had found. "But if it's one of her Oregon associates, then it could be this guy, Karl Van Mussen, local crime lord."

"If we can figure out who the swirly mist was that was trying to silence the Marchesa, that could help us figure out if this is a local situation or one that followed from the Old World," Duncan explained.

"Do we care?" Duane snorted. "The lady in black is the one stealing kids. We know this. We need to stop her. The Marchesa is incidental."

"But we don't know who she is. Or why she's drowning kids." Paige threw her hands up in exasperation. "Possibly even the Marchesa's kids, might I add."

"Yeah. To stop her we need to understand what's going on," Duncan said.

"Well." All eyes went to Nelson. "The local legends clearly all had it wrong. But the legend of a sorrowful woman emerging from water as an entity to be feared is as old as time. Perhaps we make general assumptions about her situation and just handle it?"

"What kind of assumptions?" Paige asked.

Nelson shrugged. "Like La Llorona, for example. Her legend is that she killed her kids out of anger at her husband. And then felt bad for killing them, so she spends all eternity trying to replace the kids she murdered."

"So, you're saying we just call her La Llorona and call it a day?" Duncan asked. "I don't know. Doesn't feel right."

Nelson shrugged again. "It was just an idea."

"I think we might be closer than we think." Paige leaned in. "Either the woman in black followed them all from Italy, which is possible. I mean, it does seem like the Marchesa was running after her husband died. Or she got caught up in something she shouldn't have here in Oregon."

"You're forgetting the third option," Duane added while barely moving a muscle. "The Marchesa and the woman in black are completely unrelated."

Paige frowned. "Then we'll be back where we started. No where."

Duncan pointed at the sepia-colored printouts. "No, I don't think so. This swirly mist guy is related somehow. I just know it. Why else would he have been mad she was talking? He's connected somehow."

"So we talk to the swirly mist? That's our next

move?" Paige asked, looking around at her team for confirmation and agreement.

"I like it," Nelson announced with a huge grin. "Séance again?"

"This might surprise you, but I want to try something new," Duncan responded, rubbing his chin. "Thermal camera and the spirit box. If we couldn't even capture him on film and barely saw him with our own eyes, I think he's a slippery one."

Duane groaned dramatically.

"You don't want to use the thermal camera, Duane?" Duncan asked.

"It's not that. I'm just annoyed that we have to deal with three ghosts and a river. What happened to good old-fashioned haunted houses?" He rolled his eyes to accentuate the point.

"I don't know that anything is ever as simple as it seems," Nelson said as if it provided any clarity for the team.

"Well, we don't have to like it. But it's what we've got," Duncan responded.

"And we're talking about a scared family who watched their young son be kidnapped and almost killed by an entity. Three ghosts or no, we have to solve this case for the Mellin family." Paige put her hands on her hips in a very motherly way. They would either agree or she'd scold them into it.

No one argued.

"So tonight?" Nelson asked.

"Tonight," Duncan confirmed. "Everyone rest up for a bit and we'll meet back down here in a few hours. It could be a long night."

And before they knew it, they were gathering in the lobby to head again to the banks of the Willamette River. Duane confirmed he had all the necessary equipment, and they drove to the site, Duncan and Paige in the old Chevy, Nelson and Duane in the P.I.L. van.

Paige felt redeemed that the Marchesa was found to be innocent of the crimes history had laid at her feet, but it didn't get them any closer to solving the case and ending the reign of terror caused by the Woman in the River. Perhaps tonight they would get the answers they needed.

Starting with a sighting of the swirly mist guy.

Paige felt confident if they could identify him, they could take some good guesses at the storyline. At least, they would know if it was something that followed from the Old World or started in the New.

Duane hurriedly set up the thermal cameras while Paige set up for another séance. Nelson grabbed the handheld camera, to capture some good old-fashioned footage. While they worked, they were mostly quiet. A team on a mission.

As a soft drizzle of rain began to fall, Duane thought to himself that he wanted to wrap the case so they could head to a dryer climate. He felt constantly sticky and wet here, like a cat that got caught in the sprinklers.

"Brrr…" Paige grabbed her arms and shivered. "I'm freezing."

"It's not that cold out here, Paige," Duane groaned at her complaining.

"I could really use a jacket. I thought a

sweatshirt would be fine. It's in the sixties," Paige explained, her teeth chattering between sentences.

"I don't think it's the temperature." Duncan gestured behind Paige and everyone turned.

Standing right beside Paige was the same small boy they had seen the other day. He was pale, a slight bluish color, with short pants and a shirt no one had worn in a hundred years.

"It's the boy from last night!" Paige shouted to her team. They all watched as she knelt down to his level. "Are you the Marchesa's son? What is your name?"

Paige watched as he moved his lips, but she couldn't hear any sound. "I can't hear him. Quick! Someone get the spirit box!" Paige instructed.

It was Nelson who complied. Digging in the equipment bag, much to Duane's chagrin, he whipped out the device and ran it to Paige.

As she turned it on, the familiar static of disconnected airwaves echoed through the evening air.

"Are you the Marchesa's son?" Paige asked.

Static was her only answer. "What's your name?"

Static. A pop. "William." Fuzz and more static.

Paige turned back to Nelson. "William doesn't sound very Italian."

Static. "Escape." A loud pop.

"You escaped? With the Marchesa?" Paige asked, eyes wide.

Static. "Took." Fuzz and a pop. "Safe." More static.

Nelson pointed out to the middle of the river. "Hurry. The swirly guy is back."

With a frenetic urgency, Paige asked, "What did you escape? What was it you were saved from?"

"He's coming!" The swirly mist, just as it had to the Marchesa the night before, gathered intensity and beelined for the river's edge.

"William, tell me!" Paige begged.

Static. "Mother Leona." Static, pop and then silence.

The boy and the swirly-mist ghost were gone the second the swirly ghost hit land.

The investigators all stood in silence for a moment processing the events which had just taken place. And then Paige turned off the spirit box.

"Please tell me you got everything on the camera, Duane." Paige marched up the hill to her co-investigator.

Duane rolled his eyes. "You know I did. But this is a thermal camera, so details will be in heat-mapped color waves."

"That's good. I want to see the swirly-mist guy better. Rewind it," Paige instructed.

Duane did as he was told and the team gathered over his shoulder to look at the small preview screen, watching as the swirly mist gathered over the river, took a more humanoid shape, and then barreled for the little boy named William.

And then all the colors of the shapes were gone. Vanished into the night.

"Does that look more like the Italian? Or the Oregon thug?" Nelson asked Paige and Duncan.

"We'll need to do a better analysis, but I'm

leaning Italian best friend," Duncan answered.

"The Marchesa helped William escape. She must have brought the boys out west with her in an effort to save them," Paige added.

"Save them from what exactly?" Duane asked.

"Mother Leona. Whoever that is." Paige frowned as the puzzle pieces kept tricking you into thinking that they fit but then didn't just quite.

"Why don't we ask her?" Duncan suggested. "You have the séance set up. Let's call Mother Leona."

"Will we believe anything she says?" Nelson asked.

Duncan shrugged. "I don't know. But if we can at least get some basic information out of her, we can find out who she is."

"Besides a kidnapper," Duane added.

"We don't know for sure that Mother Leona is the one kidnapping kids," Duncan responded.

"But it seems likely that she's the woman in black that everyone has accused the Marchesa of being," Paige said.

Duncan nodded. "Let's be sure."

With a salute to her tall boss, Paige marched back down to the séance. This time, Duane went with the team down to the river's edge, grabbing the handheld from Nelson. "Gimme that. You didn't even use it last time."

Paige lit all the candles as Duane filmed. Nelson, finding himself not as useful without the handheld but seeing no reason to argue with Duane, set up the concoction that helped amplify the call to spirits.

When everything was in place, Paige turned to Duncan. "Will you do the honors?"

With a nod, Duncan joined Nelson and Paige in the circle, grabbing each one of their hands. Between Nelson and Paige, however, was a large gap.

"Duane. Get over here," Paige instructed.

"I'm filming."

"We need you," Paige argued.

"Three's plenty."

Duncan jumped in to quell the argument. "It's okay, Paige. I've done it with three." He shrugged. "I've done it with even less than that, to be honest."

With a heavy sigh, Paige responded, "Fine." And she grabbed Nelson's other hand. It was a small circle but it would have to do. It *was* nice to know that they'd have everything captured on film.

Duncan recited the call of the séance, summoning the mysterious Mother Leona to the circle. He wasn't entirely sure what to expect. He had learned many years ago that a summoning didn't necessarily bring the results you wanted. You called spirits and spirits came. Sometimes the ones you want. Sometimes the ones you *don't* want.

But they were desperate enough for answers on this case that Duncan was more than willing to take the chance. Who were all these ghosts?

"Who dares to call my spirit from its rest?" A small glimmer accompanied the voice, but mostly to the naked eye it was a disembodied voice.

Which worked fine for Duncan.

"Are you Mother Leona?" Duncan asked the voice.

Laughter. "That's indeed what the children called me."

"Which children?"

"The orphans. The orphans in my care."

"Here in Oregon? Or in New York?" Duncan asked again.

A hissing sound was the response. And then, "Both."

Paige leaned over to Duncan. "Ask her how she knew William."

Another hiss. "I can hear you, girl. William was my charge."

"What about the Marchese and Marchesa?" Nelson asked. "How did you know them?"

"They were ignorant fools!" With the anger, the manifestation of Mother Leona got a little more apparent.

"Ignorant of what exactly?" Duncan asked.

"They needed to be dealt with."

Duncan exchanged a glance with Paige as Nelson adjusted his glasses and asked, "Um. How exactly did you deal with them?"

Laughter was the only response.

"That's what I thought," Nelson muttered.

"But why, Mother Leona?" Paige yelled at the almost visible ghost before her. "What made them a problem to be dealt with?"

In an instant, Mother Leona was in solid form, her veiled face inches from Paige's own. This was clearly the Woman in the River as it had been described. This woman was in a long, solid black dress, her features only slightly visible behind the veil. It was easy to see how they could've had trouble identifying her.

Paige startled at the ghost's confrontation, watching her smile behind the veil grow more sinister. But there was fire in her eyes. "Some people should go away and mind their own business."

And then she was gone. Even the air all around them felt lighter and empty.

Paige just stood there processing the ghost's ominous words. "Well!"

"I'll say one thing for tonight." Duncan put his

hands in the pockets of his baggy jeans. The temperature was dropping, and this time it was the cold, wet Portland air more than spiritual manifestations. "There's no doubt now who the Woman in the River is."

Nelson nodded and folded his arms. "We should go tell Nathan at the museum. He's spreading falsehoods to the community."

"I think it's pretty obvious what we need to do, guys." Duane shoved the camera into Nelson's hands and began cleaning up the séance. "We need to stop that bitch before she takes any more kids."

Chapter 11 - Angry Mother

"This is what I found out about her. This is Mother Leona." Paige spread the printouts on the coffee table in the lobby of their hotel. "Leona Abram. She ran an orphanage in the Lower East Side of Manhattan. It looks like she followed the Marchesa out west. It was only a few months after she left New York that Leona shows up also in Oregon."

"So clearly she was up to no good, right? Were there any accusations against her conduct with the orphans?" Duncan asked.

Paige nodded. The other investigators listened, although Duane had his hoodie up and was slouched so low it was hard to know for sure.

"Yep. I found one article accusing her of kidnapping children to put in the orphanage."

"Why would she feel the need to do that?" Nelson asked.

"Greed," Paige answered. "She could adopt them out to rich Manhattanites and pocket the money."

"Disgusting." The shock Nelson felt was plastered across his face.

"Yes, very," Paige agreed. "She could take kids from the poor families with no means to retaliate, half of whom found it to be a bit of a relief when they had one less mouth to feed. And then charge exorbitant rates to the rich, childless couples. That was her scheme."

"Did the rich couples know? Were they complicit?" Duncan asked.

Paige shook her head. "Doesn't sound like it. They thought they were adopting true orphans."

"So how do the Marchese and his wife become involved?" Nelson asked. All the investigators, except Duane, were leaning in, hanging on to every word of the sordid tale.

Paige smiled. "You can probably take a guess who one of the rich couples that wanted to adopt a child was."

"So they, what? Go to Mother Leona asking for a child and expose her operation? And how does William tie into all this? Was he one of the kids?" Duncan asked, rubbing his chin.

"The newspaper doesn't list them explicitly," Paige answered. "But they *are* listed in the adoption records. They adopted two boys. Two sons."

Duane scoffed. "If they adopted them legally, even if they were originally kidnapped, then they did nothing wrong as far as they knew. Why would Mother Leona be following them across the country? Makes no sense."

"That part isn't in anything I could find." Paige frowned as she spoke. "But I do have a theory."

Duncan gestured to her. "Let's hear it."

Paige scooted in and spoke conspiratorially, as if this were some big secret happening now and not a random theory from centuries past. "Okay. The Marchese was on to her." And then she shrugged.

"That's it? That's your big theory?" Duane asked.

"It does make sense," Nelson agreed. "The Marchese accuses Mother Leona. She worries about being exposed. She has him killed. And then the Marchesa flees out west to escape a similar fate."

Duncan continued rubbing his face in thought. "But then why would Mother Leona come out west? She had a lucrative business going on. Why leave it all behind to chase down one lady?"

Paige shrugged again. "Maybe the Marchesa threatened to expose her?"

Nelson pointed at Paige. "Money. It has to be money. You said she was greedy."

"Duane, pull up the footage of the Italian best friend," Duncan instructed.

With little urgency, Duane sighed and opened his laptop. He queued up the thermal footage of the swirly-mist ghost and pressed play.

"This guy." Duncan pointed at the screen. "This guy is the lynchpin. I just know it."

"The Italian best friend?" Paige asked. "We think he betrayed his friendship after everything they'd been through?"

"Money and fear of jail can be a powerful motivator." Nelson adjusted his glasses as he dared to justify such a turn.

"Well, I can see how choosing Mother Leona and her crime ring over your best friend could end things badly," Paige said, shifting in her seat to face Nelson. "But to kill your best friend and then chase his wife across the country? It can't just be greed."

"He was obviously her henchman," Duane said, shaking his head beneath his hoodie. "He went wherever Mother Leona sent him. And *that* likely was greed."

"So they escape their fates together in Italy after their failed rebellion," Duncan counted the facts on his fingers. "The best friend finds himself in a lucrative, even if evil, crime syndicate trafficking poor children. He tricks his best friend, the Marchese, into adopting children. The Marchese dies—"

"Is murdered," Paige corrected.

"Or so we believe, right? I don't think the

original article said murder for sure," Duncan countered.

Paige rifled through the papers until she found the original article. And then frowned. "I suppose you're right. The article doesn't say anything about murder." Scanning the article again, she froze when an idea clicked into place. "Wait a minute. The article also did not list any sons at the time of the Marchese's death."

"Did you print a copy of the adoption papers?" Duncan asked, picking up a paper as if he had any clue where the adoption papers might be.

"Did I print the adoption papers?" Paige shook her head, her short brown hair bouncing with the movement. "I really thought you knew me better than that by now. Of course I did." With swift, purposeful movements, she procured the document in question.

"So indeed, the Marchesa adopted the two boys on her own after her husband's mysterious and untimely death." Duncan let the paper drift slowly back to the table, where Nelson could see and confirm there was only one parent listed as the adoptive parent.

"So maybe the Marchese did die of tuberculosis or something. It wouldn't be unheard of at that time in history," Nelson theorized.

"Now *that* would be a fun ghost to investigate," Duane responded.

"I still think he knew too much and was murdered." Paige folded her arms across her chest, physically supporting her own theory.

"I suppose that could be true." Duncan rubbed his chin in thought. "But also I am not sure he matters all that much. What we need to know is why Mother Leona followed the Marchesa, with the best friend, out to Oregon territory. She left a profitable—and despicable—business in New York to chase down one of her clients. And then spends all eternity trying to drown children in the river." He snapped his fingers. "There's something missing there. Something big."

"Does the Italian best friend have a name?" Nelson asked Paige.

Duane scoffed. "What does that have to do with

anything?"

Nelson shrugged. "I just think it would be easier to discuss the situation if we knew his name."

Staring down Duane, Paige answered Nelson. "Yes, he has a name. Giovanni De Luca. He was a founder of the Young Italy party with Luigi di Ragnoni, the Marchese."

"It seems pretty clear that the Marchesa was running, possibly trying to save her two sons somehow. But we need to know why Giovanni and Mother Leona followed. And then killed them." Duncan looked around at his team for answers but received blank stares in return.

Paige twisted her lips in thought before stating, "I didn't find much about them out here in Oregon. I mean, everyone out here thought the Lady in the River was the Marchesa all this time."

"We have to ask the Marchesa what happened," Nelson added. "Or perhaps William. Mother Leona and her Italian henchman are not to be trusted."

"And that's what I've been saying," Duane

muttered.

"It's a simple question, really. What exactly transpired that triggered Mother Leona so badly?" Duncan added.

"I think we'll get further with William." Paige nodded to the group.

"You know we can't always conjure who we want," Duane responded.

"Man. I'm not looking forward to it." Duncan rubbed his chin.

"What?" Nelson asked him.

"Doing another séance by the river. It's cold here," Duncan answered.

Paige laughed. "You're just mad because you have to put on shoes." She gestured to his flip-flop-covered feet and freely wiggling toes.

Duncan smirked. "I don't deny that."

"It's more than cold, Duncan," Duane added. "The séance outside might be impossible. We may need to get creative. It's supposed to rain tonight."

Duncan stood and stretched his back. "Then

everyone dress warm. Wear shoes and a coat. Bring umbrellas. Tonight, we find out what's going on and why Mother Leona is kidnapping children and drowning them for all eternity."

Duane snapped his laptop shut. "So we can send that bitch back to hell where she belongs."

A few hours later they were gathering to head to the river for another go. The rain outside had already picked up from a light drizzle and now smacked the hotel front window with fat drops.

"What's the plan for dealing with the rain?" Duane asked.

"I think I do prefer ghost-hunting inside haunted locations. Dealing with the elements is tricky," Nelson added, although he neglected to provide any real substantive answer to Duane's question.

"We're going to use two methods," Duncan instructed. "Paige will use the EVP recorder in case we can get answers to our question." He then lifted and shook a flashlight for the team to see. "I will ask yes or no questions and we'll have William or the Marchesa—

whoever will talk to us—manipulate the energy to answer."

Duane rolled his eyes. "I guess I wasn't clear. How do you plan to keep everything dry?"

"Umbrellas." Duncan shrugged.

Paige looked at Duane like he was a child. "We may not be used to rain, Duane. But we'll protect the equipment. You just use the handheld under an umbrella and with any luck, the rain slows."

A crack of lightning responded to Paige's statement. Nelson raised an eyebrow but said nothing more.

"We're going to have to earn this one," Duane muttered. The thunder roared in agreement.

It was a short drive, although visibility was light and the roads were slick. The team drove slowly out to the river as the sky continued to battle them. Unsurprisingly, no one was on the road and the riverbank was empty and dark.

Paige's foot slipped on the muddy walk down the hill and had to stick her arms out for balance, barely avoiding a hard fall. The rain was pouring all around them, dropping off the edges of their umbrellas like large coins.

The lightning flashed again.

"I feel very vulnerable right now," Paige said to anyone and everyone. The only response was the rumble of thunder.

Duncan gestured at Paige and then shouted to be heard above the elements. "You ready to record?"

Wiping her wet hand on her wet jeans, she nodded and then pulled the small silver EVP device from her pocket.

Duncan moved the flashlight in his hand this way and that. "I originally had thought about placing the flashlight on the ground, but clearly that isn't going to work." He looked all around himself for a solution whereby the ghosts could manipulate the light freely.

"What's the idea now, genius?" Duane prompted.

Duncan shrugged. "I guess I just hold it. Duane, hit record."

When the red light on the handheld camera was going, Duncan turned the flashlight off and they all stood in the dark. By the fast-moving river. In a rainstorm.

It was eerie.

"We're hoping to communicate with William, the ghost of the little boy taken by Mother Leona," Duncan called out into the night. "Or the Marchesa di Rignoni, who might have been murdered by Mother Leona."

Lightning flashed and the rain continued to descend all around them. They were mostly dry under their umbrellas, but not completely.

"You can answer me by flashing this light in my hand. Once for yes, twice for no," Duncan shouted into the night, looking all around himself in case he could see the ghosts he was hoping for. "Are you here?"

Rain continued to pour but nothing happened with the flashlight. They just stood there for a few seconds getting soaked, the umbrellas providing a modicum of protection.

"Why did Mother Leona kill you?" Paige shouted into the storm.

"He can't answer a question like that with 'once for yes and twice for no,' Paige." Duane rolled his eyes, his handheld camera continuing to film.

"I have the EVP recorder, Duane." Paige fought the urge to stick her tongue out at him.

"Just ask yes or no questions," Duane argued.

Paige opened her mouth to yell back, but she stopped when the lightning flashed and in the brief moment of illumination, they could see the gray ghost of a young boy.

William.

"Quiet, you two," Duncan instructed. "He's here."

"Did Mother Leona murder you?" Paige asked.

Duncan gestured to his flashlight. "Once for yes, twice for no." The light flashed very briefly once. Then stopped. Was the flashlight even working right? A moment later, the thunder rumbled.

"Was she your actual mother?" Nelson shouted

into the night. Two flashes. Maybe the flashlight was okay?

"So you were a victim of kidnapping?" Duncan asked. One flash.

"We don't understand why she followed you out here?" Paige asked, the din of the rain drumming all around them threatening to drown out her voice. "Why did she want you and your brother so badly?"

Another flash of lightning and William appeared inches from Paige's umbrella, the sudden sight of the ghost causing her to jump. "It was me. It was always me."

No device needed. They could hear him.

"Was she using her for a curse?" Paige asked the ghost boy standing right in front of her.

"We need to hurry," Nelson shouted. "I see the swirly ghost on the water. Giovanni de Luca. He's here."

The ghost boy shook his head no. "It was me."

"What was you, William? I don't understand." Paige responded.

"He's coming this way!" Nelson warned Paige as

the swirly ghost became more than mist and formed the henchman, Giovanni. And then it headed straight for William.

"I killed her. To pay for her sins. She thought killing me would end it."

The thunder rumbled and William disappeared just as Giovanni approached him.

"Giovanni!" Duncan yelled to the ghost. He turned toward the investigator at the sound of his name, but he said nothing and his face remained expressionless.

His eyes were a dark void, as if death itself lived there. His manifestation was just a shell and the rest of his soul remained on the other side. Duncan shivered and it wasn't just from the cold.

"Were you cursed too?" Duncan asked.

Two large steps later and Giovanni stood inches from Duncan's face, nearly mirroring Duncan in size. And then he shook his head no and disappeared.

"This is no good. No good at all." Duncan shook his head.

"What do you mean? We got good intel," Nelson argued. "William was punishing Mother Leona. Now we know what to do to end the Woman in the River's reign of terror. We just have to break the cycle of revenge."

"I mean the dumb flashlight idea in the rain." Dunca hit the device a few times. "It's totally soaked and won't turn on."

Duane snorted. "It was pretty stupid."

"So what do we do now?" Paige asked.

Duncan gestured at his team. "Has anyone checked the weather forecast, by chance?"

Nelson raised his hand. "I have, of course."

"Is it supposed to rain tomorrow?" Duncan asked. Nelson shook his head no. "Then we're done for tonight before more equipment gets shot."

Lightning flashed again. This time there was no William nor Giovanni appearing in the burst of light.

"What do we do about Mother Leona?" Paige asked.

"Tonight? Nothing," Duncan answered. "But tomorrow we end this. Once and for all."

Chapter 12 - End the Reign of Terror

"So that's the truth of it. William killed her—he didn't really say how but we sort of assume drowning—and so she is on a revenge spree forever more," Duncan explained to Lucy Mellin as he and Paige sat with her in her family room by the big, sliding glass door.

Paige handed Lucy the printout that explained the accusations about Mother Leona.

"What a dark and creepy tale," Lucy answered as she took the paper. She didn't read it, just held it like she could absorb its truths. "But how did they end up in Oregon?"

"Mother Leona and her henchman followed the Marchesa out west," Duncan answered as he leaned back on the couch. Even as deep as this couch was, Duncan was somehow able to dwarf it with his large frame. "We don't know exactly why she was so obsessed with these two particular children. Perhaps the Marchesa or William had threatened her before? But that's just a guess."

"So, because she was kidnapping children, and one of those kidnapped children murdered her, she drowns kids forever more?" Lucy frowned. "That's so awful." She shook her head and then leaned in. "But more than anything, we just need to make it stop. I had always thought it was just creepy local lore. Portland is filled with ghost stories and morbid tales. I never thought much about it."

"Until the tale came true for you." Paige nodded at Lucy.

"Yes," Lucy answered with a grimace. "It's easy to ignore when it's not your child getting kidnapped, I guess."

"Don't feel guilty. How would you possibly have known?" Duncan asked. "But in our line of work, you might be surprised to find that many of these legends and stories have at least some semblances of truth to them."

"Our teammate, Nelson is right at this moment informing your local historian of the real history. At least as much as we know," Paige explained.

Duncan leaned forward, resting his elbows on his knees. "Essentially that the Woman in the River isn't the Marchesa. We want to stop the spread of that rumor. She was trying to do right by the children she adopted."

"So she must've known." For the first time Lucy looked at the papers in her hand. "She must've adopted those boys to save them."

"Yes. And then we assume she came out west to escape Mother Leona's clutches," Paige added.

"How sinister that she wanted those specific boys. I wonder why?" Lucy asked. "Doesn't that feel important?"

"It does." On that note, Duncan stood. "But for us, now that we know the reason she continues kidnapping children, we know how to stop it. So that's what we're going to do tonight."

Lucy stood to match her guests. "How on earth

do you do that?"

Duncan smiled. "We break the cycle."

Lucy shook her head. "I suppose it's enough that the threat will be gone. It's all we wanted from the start. We want to be able to sleep at night again."

With thank-you's and assurances of soon-to-come peace, Duncan and Paige left Lucy to begin their night stopping the Woman in the River.

They had barely turned the engine in Duncan's old Chevy when Duncan's phone rang. "Talk to me, Duane."

"Duncan. There's more. There's a whole lot more."

Duncan looked at Paige who could only shrug. "What do you mean there's more?"

Duane sighed so heavily through the phone, Duncan could practically hear him rolling his eyes. "I was listening to Paige's device, which surprisingly remained pretty intact despite the weather. You guys gotta hear this for yourselves. Come back to my room now."

After hanging up and pulling out into traffic, Duncan gave a quick rundown to Paige. On their way back to the hotel, Paige filled Nelson in and it wasn't long before they were all in Duane's dark room, squeezed in sitting around his laptop.

"I put the audio onto my computer so you could hear it better," Duane explained as they all looked at a simple black box on screen with some green bars that went up and down in line with the sound.

He pressed play.

At first it was static and the sound of rushing water, most likely the pounding rain they had experienced. Duncan shivered at the memory of being so wet and cold. But then a voice came through. And it was female.

The Marchesa.

They hadn't heard her that night or seen her at all. They'd been clueless of her presence.

"Please understand. As long as William doesn't rest, I am unable to rest. I must protect him." They heard the Marchesa's voice louder than everything else, as if she had her lips up against the microphone and they hadn't even been aware.

"A mother to the end." Paige clutched her heart at the sweetness of a mother's love.

"He's right," the Marchesa continued. "It has always been about William."

Duane pressed pause and then explained, "It's hard to hear but I think this aligns with when William was telling us he killed Mother Leona. Which sounded dark and evil last night, but not as much after hearing this."

Duncan nodded to Duane in acknowledgement, but also in encouragement to continue the recording.

There was some static and a pop. Then a rumble of thunder before they heard the Marchesa's voice again, loud and clear. "She always wanted William, that evil woman. She was grooming him to be her scout. She knew Giovanni wouldn't be able to much longer, as he was already getting so old that the kids didn't always trust him."

They heard Duncan's voice far off in the

distance, as if he hadn't been mere feet from Paige. "Giovanni!"

"He's nothing. He just fell victim to easy money. And Henry too, William's younger brother. My baby son. They were both innocent collateral in her quest for William." The Marchesa continued speaking into the microphone.

In the background, very faintly, they could hear themselves talking about calling it all off.

"Mother Leona's death was an accident. When she found us, she kept watch from a distance for a while. And then after she'd murdered me and Henry, she was able to get William alone. She cornered him on a bridge and tried to grab him. He struggled and pushed her off, but she fell from the bridge and drowned. He never meant to hurt her. He just wanted to be free. I just wanted both my boys to be rid of—" The recording ended.

"What? Where's the rest?" Duncan asked.

Duane pointed a thumb at Paige. "She turned it off."

Paige held her hands up. "What? I didn't know. I thought we were done for the night."

"Well, the Marchesa is proving to be a great ally," Nelson stated, adjusting his glasses. "So now we know Mother Leona's obsession with William. And how she died."

Paige nodded. "And that she can finally be at rest when we put William's soul to rest."

"And it sounds like Giovanni can also rest when Mother Leona is put to rest," Duane added.

"Back to Mother Leona. She is the center of this wheel, both when she was alive and now in her death." Duncan stood up. "I don't want to wait for tonight. Let's head to the river now."

"You just don't want to be cold." Paige smirked as she spoke.

Duncan shrugged. "A little bit that. But also, I feel like Mother Leona's reign of terror has gone on long enough. Kidnapping for a century and a half, trying to drown kids. Actually drowning for sure the Marchesa and Henry. Enough is enough."

"I love it when we get fired up." Duane stood and pulled his hoodie up over his bald, tattooed head. "Let's go. Let's do this."

"Let's put some souls to rest," Paige smiled.

"It's what we do," Nelson added.

"Nelson, I'm going to need a ceremony or incantation for a soul seeking vengeance in the afterlife," Duncan instructed.

"I was researching that earlier today, actually," Nelson answered. "It's called 'lustratio.' It basically strips the need for vengeance from their soul. If we remove that from Mother Leona, it should be fairly straightforward to put the remaining souls to rest. They are all so fixated on her that none of them can cross over yet. Like a spiritual train of sorts. They're all connected, but in this case the engine can't stop circling in one spot."

"The engineer is a kidnapper and murderess." Duane scowled at the mere thought of Mother Leona.

"Lustratio it is." Duncan clapped his hands together. "So what do we need?"

Nelson responded, "The usual. Candles. Salt. Oh! This one requires mustard seeds."

Duncan rubbed his chin. "That is a new one. We might need to do a mustard seed run."

"Nope," Duane answered. "Got it."

"Then let's go stop some kidnappings, shall we?" Duncan asked.

This time of day, the river wasn't as empty as it had been the last few days. The sky was cloudy, but it wasn't cold and the water hadn't yet formed into drizzle-filled air. It seemed to Duncan to be the best weather conditions they had encountered since being in Portland. He longed for the sunshine back in Southern California that would allow him to cruise around in his flip-flops once again.

But he had to also admit that the view of the fast-moving Willamette River with trees everywhere you looked was beautiful and serene. He made mental note to one day come and enjoy Portland without having to work putting vengeful spirits to rest.

"Let's head down this way a bit where it's less

crowded." Duncan gestured away from the main area where they had parked. It wasn't packed like a summer day, but there were half a dozen families playing near the water or sitting on a bench and enjoying a hot drink. He wasn't necessarily worried about them seeing the ceremony, but he didn't want to have to stop and give a ton of explanation. He wanted to put souls to rest and end the legend of the Woan in the River.

And stop the chances of another boy like Keenan being taken in the night.

When they had reached a more secluded area, Duane dropped the big black bag with all the supplies. Bushes and brush grew nearly to the water's edge, so there wasn't much riverbank this afternoon for a big set-up. "Tell me what to do, Nelson."

"We're going to need a line of candles resting atop a line of salt. That's for protection, but also for the light of the afterlife that we want Mother Leona eventually to go to," Nelson explained. "Then we each hold handfuls of salt and mustard seeds."

Duane raised an eyebrow. "That's it?"

Nelson nodded. "Yes. Lustratio is mostly power of the words."

"We should probably hurry," Duncan instructed. "We know how this goes. The swirly-mist ghost and Mother Leona aren't going to sit idly by."

"Hurrying," Duane responded.

"I'll get the salt and mustard seeds for us while you do the candles, Duane," Paige said, while rummaging in the black bag. Duane stared at her for a moment but said nothing before resuming his task.

It was less than a minute later that they stood behind the line of candles and salt, ready to begin the ceremony.

"We need the words, Nelson," Duncan stated.

Paige tapped her leg. "And you'd better hurry. Giovanni is here now, I think." With a salt-filled hand, she indicated the river where a fog was rolling off the water. Otherwise, the air was clear, so it did seem ominous to the investigators.

Anyone else would probably suspect it was just a simple fog.

"Yes, yes. Everyone lean over my phone. I have the words pulled up. And then we repeat them three times before throwing first the salt and then the mustard seed at Mother Leona."

"Nelson, I'm so proud of you," Paige squealed. "You brought your phone."

Ignoring Paige, Duncan asked, "What if we don't see Mother Leona? Can we throw everything at Giovanni?"

"We may have to. I think he's coming this way," Duane said with zero inflection.

"Don't worry. I have the salt and mustard seed right here at my feet. I can get us more if we need to battle more than one ghost," Paige answered.

"Now, remember. This just removes the vengefulness of the spirit. We'll still have to help them cross over," Nelson explained.

"Can we just get to it? He's coming." Duane gestured at the river where the gentle fog had formed the outline of a human and had begun floating toward them.

"Okay, here. Lean in." Nelson held up his phone for all to read.

Purifica cor meum

Animam ultione liberare

Da mihi pacem

In unison, the team read the words together. As they did, the swirly-mist ghost of Giovanni de Luca continued floating toward them. But he stopped abruptly in front of the salt, his swirly face barely formed by the fog that created his being. He was unable to advance further.

So they read the words again.

"Look! I think it's working!" Paige shouted as she pointed at the face of the ghost of Giovanni, the henchman of Mother Leona in life and in death.

"Let's say the words again. They seem to be softening his soul, at least," Duncan said.

But he had barely finished his sentence when the misty formation of Giovanni's ghost was swiped in two, like a gust of air parting smoke fumes.

And there, behind where Giovanni had stood,

was a figure dressed all in black, anger and hatred pouring off of her with such strength, Duncan was sure he could actually *see* those emotions.

"Say the words again!" Duncan yelled with urgency.

Purifica cor meum

Animam ultione liberare

Da mihi pacem

"I think we need to throw the salt and mustard seeds now," Nelson calmly explained.

"At who? Giovanni or Leona?" Paige asked.

Mother Leona began advancing toward them from where she stood on the river's edge. She moved slowly, but with anger and purpose. Nelson knew she wasn't coming toward them for a casual conversation. She wanted blood. Or, more likely, drowning. But she, too, was blocked by the line of salt.

"Both of them!" Nelson answered. And it was good enough for the team. They threw their handfuls of salt first, then mustard seed, as Nelson had previously instructed.

The ghost of Giovanni de Luca re-formed and, next to the angry ghost of The Woman in the River, he stood in full apparition. He held a newsboy cap in his hand, so clear and well-formed that Nelson could make out the herringbone pattern of the material. Nelson looked from Giovanni's ghost to Mother Leona's and suddenly wished he had his EMF detector. He was speculating that these readings were next level, especially for a haunting next to a riverbank.

But it was Paige who was able to gather her senses and get the job done. "Giovanni!"

He turned sad eyes to her, eyes brimming with the emotions that can only come from a lifetime of regret. If you could weigh his expression, it would break the scale.

"It's time. Go to the light," Paige instructed, matching the ghost's expression with an equal amount of compassion.

But the words stoked another reaction in Mother Leona. She screeched like a wild woman and reached for her henchman. Only this time, instead of dissipating into puffs of smoke, he stood there completely unaware of Mother Leona's flailing.

He kept his eyes locked on Paige.

"It's working, Paige," Duncan encouraged. "The lustratio ceremony has softened his heart. Mother Leona is powerless over him now."

"Go to the light. It's here for you."

Nelson reached over to Paige and handed her some mustard seeds. "Can't hurt."

With a shrug, Paige took the mustard seeds and gently tossed them toward Giovanni's ghost. "It's time to go home."

With sad, remorseful eyes, Giovanni began to fade from view.

And this only made Mother Leona screech all the more. She was angry, reaching out bony fingers toward the investigators. The only saving grace was that she couldn't cross the line of salt and candles.

"Well, it worked for the henchman," Paige announced.

Nelson began handing out salt and mustard

seeds to everyone again. "We have to do another round for Mother Leona. Giovanni was probably more contrite over his actions. That made him more pliable."

As the investigators gathered around Nelson's phone and read the chanting of the lustratio once again, Mother Leona kept screeching and reaching. It felt so loud to Paige, but when she looked over to the families playing at the river, they were completely ignorant of what was happening around the bend.

Good. She had no idea how they would explain what was going on over here to families with young children, the likes of which Mother Leona liked to kidnap and drown.

But before she could look back at the angry ghost of the woman dressed in black who had been torturing Portland for centuries, the screeching instantly stopped. For a moment, Paige thought the Lustratio was working. But when she saw the ghost of William, she knew it was his presence.

"William, no! Just go to the light!" Paige yelled at the young boy.

And then the Marchesa appeared beside him. She spoke to Paige, although she was focused on Mother Leona. "This is something he must do. For his own soul to have peace."

"Mother Leona." William spoke low, controlled. If Paige was just passing by, it would seem like nothing more than the wind picking up off the river.

Mother Leona's howl in response, however, was a little harder to disguise. She was angry. And fighting. And perhaps a little sad? Maybe the lustratio *was* working, and her vengeance was morphing into regret.

William stepped forward. Surprisingly, Mother Leona did not attack him. "Mother Leona, I forgive you. Can you forgive me?"

Mother Leona opened her mouth wider than a natural mouth should go and let out another screech. The sound of her anguish flew through the air like a bird of prey seeking its next victim.

Another step forward and William stretched out a hand to the howling woman in black. "It's over, Mother Leona. You did what you had to do to survive.

And so did I."

Another step and he was directly in front of Mother Leona. She continued screeching but did not physically try to grab him or restrain him. William grabbed both her hands in his. "I forgive you."

And the screeching stopped. They stood for a moment holding hands, the young boy she kidnapped and the woman he killed.

And then Nelson shouted. "The salt and seeds!"

As if coming out of a daydream, his words jolted the rest of the investigators. It wasn't in perfect unison, but they all threw the mustard seeds and salt they were holding in their hands at the pair of ghosts in front of them.

A small smile danced across William's lips as they both slowly faded from view.

Paige sighed. "They're gone. I can feel the shift in energy."

Duncan gestured. "The Marchesa is still here."

In an instant, she disappeared from where she was standing and reappeared directly in front of the salt line. "Thank you."

It was only after she disappeared again that Duncan nodded and said, "You're welcome."

Paige jumped in the air and clapped her hands together. "It worked! Honestly, I was a little skeptical, Nelson. But we did it!"

"Yes, there were a number of permutations that could have altered the way this case ended." Nelson adjusted his black-rimmed glasses.

"Let's not give ourselves any prizes," Duane muttered as he began blowing out the candles. "These ghosts were exhausted and ready to cross over."

"Yes, well, whatever the reason, I'm glad there will be no more kidnappings by the Woman in the River in Portland. That is satisfying," Duncan responded.

They hadn't had much to set up for the ceremony, so it didn't take them long to clean everything up and begin walking back to the P.I.L. van.

And as they walked by the families, one man watched them with a side eye. Paige could swear they actually felt the new energy in the air now that the legend that haunted their nightmares was finally gone.

Chapter 13 – That's a Wrap!

Lucy and Joe Mellin sat on their couch listening to the investigators. What little light was left of the day was creeping in through their sliding glass door. The room was dark except for the soft light of a lamp on an end table. It hadn't started raining yet, but Duncan felt the promise of it brewing outside. He longed for his dingy apartment back home in Southern California, where no one was yelling at him for wearing flip-flops throughout the year.

Duncan drowned the armchair he sat in across from the Mellins. He clapped his hands together in finality as he said, "I don't think you need to worry about the Woman in the River anymore. Her days of kidnapping and drowning are behind her."

"But how can you be sure?" Lucy reached for her husband's hand and squeezed, her desire to believe warring with her anxiety.

"The truth is, we can't be completely," Duncan explained truthfully.

"But we saw her soften her hold on this world and I felt her energy change, which I associate with crossing over," Paige leaned in to explain, sensing that Lucy needed some type of assurance in order to sleep at night. Nelson and Duane waited outside in the van.

"I don't know how we can ever thank you," Joe answered, the weight of the whole ordeal showing plainly in the weariness on his face. You could practically hold nickels in his worry lines. "This has been a complete nightmare for us. No one has slept much in weeks."

"This is what we do. Especially knowing that the Woman in the River has been terrorizing families all across the region, not just in one home. We had to give the community some peace," Duncan explained.

"And also the ghosts," Paige added. "We give their souls peace too." She smiled. "It's also what we do."

"How many ghosts were caught up in this?" Lucy

asked wide-eyed.

"A total of four," Duncan answered.

Paige used her fingers as she listed. "The Marchesa, William, Giovanni the Henchman and Mother Leona. I assume William's brother has been at peace this whole time." She shrugged. "At least we didn't see him."

"Ghosts need energy to manifest. Anger, fear, vengeance, negative emotions. Those can feed them energy and over time, they can become quite powerful." Duncan leaned his weight on one arm of the chair as he explained. "In this case, we're talking about a century and a half of a spirit in a cycle of vengeance and fear. She had become quite the force to be reckoned with."

"But that all stopped the instant William forgave her. So her cycle should now be broken." Paige bounced in her seat with the happy news.

"Well." Lucy turned sorrowful eyes toward her husband. "I suppose if William can forgive her, perhaps we can find it in our hearts to forgive her as well."

Joe looked stricken, but he didn't argue.

Duncan smiled. "Then I suppose your tale has a happy outcome after all. And taking away *your* anger and fear? That will definitely weaken her hold on this earth, if by some chance she hasn't crossed over."

"Although I'm sure she did," Paige added with a comforting smile.

Joe Mellin stood, extending a hand to Duncan and thereby concluding this chapter of their lives. "Well, thank you all for what you've done for us. It means more than you know."

"Oh, believe me, we've seen a lot of cases, encountered a lot of different types of entities. We know firsthand how debilitating fear can be." Duncan stood and shook Joe's hand. Paige followed, shaking first Joe's hand and then Lucy's. "And how liberating it can be to move past that. Get answers. Find resolution."

Paige pointed at Duncan. "And *that* is why we do what we do."

"You know how to find me, so call if anything else ever pops up, but I suspect you won't need to." Duncan stood with his hands on his hips, towering over everyone in the small living room.

"I hope to only have to call you to say hi," Joe answered. Lucy and Paige laughed. Duncan nodded because he knew it was no joke.

"We'll let ourselves out. You two enjoy some time as a family, knowing that no woman in black is waiting to come get your son." Duncan started walking toward the front door, Paige right behind.

With a chorus of goodbyes from the Mellins, Duncan and Paige stepped out into the crisp evening. A soft drizzle filled the air, chilling their skin with each tiny touch. The sky was covered in clouds so that it looked like gray cotton balls had created a layer of shield between them and the setting sun.

"They happy?" Duane grunted when he saw Duncan and Paige.

Duncan nodded. "Relieved."

"Good. Let's go before it starts raining." And without waiting for a response, Duane opened the driver's side door of the P.I.L. van and climbed in.

"This was an interesting case." Nelson removed

his glasses and cleaned away the condensation that had collected. "A woman and her henchman so coiled inside their evil operation that they couldn't get untangled even in death." He shook his head. "A cautionary tale."

Duncan shook his head. "Consider all of us fairly warned."

Nelson nodded as he placed his glasses back on. "See you back home."

"See you soon."

Paige waved wildly. "Be safe, guys."

Duane and Nelson left before Duncan and Paige were even in the beat-up old Chevy. But as Duncan turned the key, he gave one final glance at the Mellin house.

"Do you think Portland will miss the Woman in the River?" Duncan asked.

"Nah," Paige responded with a flick of her hand. "They'll always have their legend to scare little kids straight. Only now no kids actually have to drown to instill that fear."

"Good case," Duncan nodded. "One for the

books."

Duncan pulled away and out into the winding tree-lined street where the Mellins lived. The soft glow of a streetlight guided the way as gentle drizzle morphed into heavier rain drops.

As the rain began to fall, Duncan glanced in his rearview mirror. A final glance at the home in Portland where the Woman in the River terrorized a young family.

And they had solved the case, giving the family—and the ghosts—some peace.

Chapter 14 – The Marchesa's Story

In hindsight, I wish we had never left Italy.

At the time it felt like the only option, with mounting pressures from every side. My husband, the Marchese, felt there was no other option. To stay in the country of our birth after trying to overthrow the government—no matter how noble the cause—was certain death.

"Union, strength, and liberty!" we chanted in the streets, growing the fervor amongst our nation to free ourselves from Austrian and Papal influence and control. We just wanted an independent democratic nation like the United States. The common people were starting to join us, and our Young Italy movement was gaining ground.

But someone had talked.

Somehow the authorities had found out what we were planning, and the rebellion of 1842 was easily crushed. Many of our co-liberators were captured and thrown in prison. Only by the grace of God were my husband and I able to evade capture.

And so we had to flee.

As noble people we had lots of connections. My husband called in a favor from a British diplomat, and the next thing I knew we were on a boat for New York. I had nothing but the clothes on my back, yet at the time, it felt like more than enough. Stay and die or run with little. The latter seemed like the obvious choice.

And I had always wanted to go to America!

My parents had known some families who had previously gone to the United States and their letters home were always filled with the most wonderful things. People were free to become whatever they wanted. They danced in the streets. They were free. Of course, growing up with wealth and a title I had never longed for any of those things, but running from persecution forged them into diamonds I now longed for.

But when we arrived in New York with my husband's best friend, Giovanni, we were shuffled into the projects with all the other immigrants. All my life I had worn the highest quality jewelry and the day we left Italy was no different. I was able to sell what I had been wearing to allow Luigi and me to establish a residence.

But not all Italians were of similar means. Giovanni was penniless. The only life he had ever known was to do the bidding of noblemen. So when Mother Leona offered him a job, he felt he couldn't refuse.

And, at first, it seemed like an amazing blessing to have such secure work supporting orphans. I remember being a tiny bit jealous of Giovanni.

Our lives were simple in New York and, while I wouldn't say we flourished, I didn't hate it. We had a small place to call our own. Friends. Laughter.

The only thing I longed for was the sound of children running around our apartment laughing. But I was never given the chance before Luigi contracted consumption.

The doctors told us we needed to head out west to dryer air.

We began to ask around about settlements.

Where were people heading? Over and over we were told the Oregon Territory at the end of the Oregon Trail. But it was a long hard trip, and even healthy people had a low chance of survival. We talked about going. Even imagined together what it might be like. Sometimes Luigi had stars in his eyes as he fancied himself living in the wild west.

Just think. Two Italian nobles riding horses and fighting cowboys! Ah, the wonder of America!

But it wasn't meant to be. Luigi succumbed to his illness before we'd even packed a single thing.

In my grief, I just couldn't stand the loneliness. Giovanni saw my melancholy and encouraged me to adopt from Mother Leona. A woman who had just lost her husband and had no clue how she would continue to make a way for herself in this New World now adding children to the equation? Preposterous.

But I did it anyway. Against my rational judgment. Because the moment I saw William and Henry, I knew they were mine. It wasn't love. It wasn't pity. It was complete certainty from the Lord above that these two boys were meant to be mine.

And then the strangest thing happened. Mother Leona tried to talk me out of it.

At the time I had thought she was looking out for me, concern for a poor widow and her financial prospects. I had no idea about her dark secret that she had kidnapped these boys from a loving home with the goal of raising William as her own.

Not as her own son, mind you. Despite her title as "mother," she had no desire to actually nurture children. She was grooming him to take over her thuggery when Giovanni became too old or decided to leave her. Because I didn't know these dark thoughts of hers, I was not easily dissuaded from my own vision of life with these boys.

And no one but myself and the soul of my recently deceased husband knew that the life I envisioned was at the end of the Oregon Trail.

As a noblewoman, despite the shielding I had experienced, I knew there was one great equalizer that changed the hearts of every man and woman. I knew those children would be mine if I could wave enough money in front of Mother Leona.

I sold almost everything I had and everything my husband and I had built up here in New York. I kept a tiny bit, only what I would need to get to Oregon, and offered the rest to Mother Leona for the boys. My boys. The rest I would figure out when I got there. For some strange reason, I had no worry about how I would provide out west. I just knew I had to get there with William and Henry.

And it worked. Mother Leona took no more than ten seconds to snatch the carpet bag that contained all the money right out of my hands. And I signed the papers, grabbed the boys and left.

Yes, I saw Giovanni's face. I knew it held a dire warning. His eyes locked on mine and spoke silently of the dangerous game I was playing. And I didn't care. Let them try to find me after I left!

Leaving was easy. With my two boys in tow, I began the arduous trip out west. But for me this was a golden opportunity to live the life Luigi and I had always dreamt about when he was sick. I was doing this for him.

To me, the dusty earth was a magical oasis. The bumpy travel was a glorious ride. Even the days we had no food to eat, the rumble in our stomachs was simply a reminder that the suffering would be worth it.

And when we made it to Oregon, at first it was worth all the sacrifices.

We were welcomed with open arms. I had very few skills, but I saw another woman washing people's clothing for them and it seemed easy enough. If I did the chores no one else wanted to do and could make money to feed my sons, then I would do it happily. We set up shop, made friends, and established our new life out west.

It was a few months into this new life when Henry woke up crying one night. He had had a nightmare about the night he'd been taken by Mother Leona from his birth family. I, of course, had no idea that this had happened and Henry had been too little at the time to provide details. He just knew that he hurt deeply. That he had been scared. That he'd been taken from people who loved him.

But William remembered.

We sat by candlelight until the wee hours of the morning with William explaining to me all that had transpired and how it was that Mother Leona filled her orphanages. I was horrified. It had never occurred to me in all my life to imagine that someone would do something so damnable to make a petty buck.

And like the naïve woman that I was, I assumed Giovanni had no idea.

With all the ignorance of a small child, I sent a letter to Giovanni detailing what the boys had told me, encouraging him to escape. But of course, he'd known. He'd always known. I see that now.

He wrote back to me with news that he was joining me out west. I was elated! Even the boys were excited at the prospect of seeing a familiar face.

But he didn't come alone.

And when I saw Mother Leona, I knew everything was crashing down around me.

She and Giovanni cornered me one evening. I told the boys to run and they did. Thank God for that one grace. If I am thankful for anything, it's that my sweet boys didn't have to watch me be murdered.

Just before he shoved me under the river water, I saw the pain in Giovanni's eyes. He didn't want to hurt the wife of his once dearest friend. But he also couldn't stop. Or at least he didn't hesitate to begin my demise. Once my head was under, though, Mother Leona jumped on my back to make sure my head stayed down in the soil of the river bottom. Rocks, dirt and debris floated into my nostrils and lungs as I screamed for Giovanni to stop, to have mercy.

Although it was likely minutes only that I fought hard for my life, it had felt like an eternity. Until my soul stepped out of my body and I could see what eternity truly meant. The moment I realized that that was my lifeless body floating in the water in front of me, I looked quickly for Luigi, my beloved husband. But it was only my ghost.

My ghost, my dead body, Giovanni and Mother Leona.

I watched them as they ran away like animals, discarding my body as if it were day-old garbage. My body floated before me, lifeless. But all I could think about were my boys.

It didn't take Mother Leona long to realize she'd need to get rid of Henry too, if she wanted to take William back with her to New York. So the next day she cornered them both on a bridge that crossed the Willamette. And I know now that cornering them both was her big mistake. William suspected she had killed me, but he didn't know for sure. And certainly he wouldn't allow his thoughts to dwell on that.

But he saw her push Henry over the bridge.

And all the anger, all the bitterness at the life she'd stolen, at the children she'd victimized, and the murder of the only family he had left, it all boiled over in an instant. Without rational thought or care for the consequences, he ran at Mother Leona with everything he had and shoved her right behind Henry.

Giovanni stood at his side as they both leaned over the bridge wall to watch her helpless body cartwheel down to the river, landing with a large splash. The rushing water carried her away as she flailed her arms and swallowed river water.

By the time William regained his senses and started to run, Giovanni had already reached a strong arm toward him and grabbed hold. William fought hard. In a year or two, he probably would have been the victor. But now, as scrawny as he was, he couldn't wiggle free from Giovanni's grip.

Giovanni strangled him right there on the bridge in broad daylight and tossed him into the water.

My body, William's body and Henry's body all washed up in different places, but they knew we were a family. With no evidence whatsoever, they came to their own conclusions and assumed I had murdered my boys and killed myself. They never even guessed that the other body that would wash up on the river's edge was somehow related. They would never assume the strange man who had shown up in town was connected to all four deaths.

And so I would be the villain for more than a century and a half despite being a victim.

For her part, Mother Leona never stopped looking for William. For retribution, for finishing what she had come our west to do, for retaliation, for feeding her special brand of evil, she continued hunting and preying on local children.

And they all continued saying it was me.

Henry's soul has always been at peace. The small angel who never hurt a fly and simply longed for the life he'd once known with his biological family. It is the one small blessing of my afterlife that he went directly to heaven when his time on earth was through.

William, however, couldn't rest. And I wouldn't rest until he did.

There was guilt and shame, knowing he had taken a life even if that life was an evil one. And the continued kidnappings even in Mother Leona's death. All this weighed on William's soul.

But finally, after all this time, he has learned to forgive. He's forgiven Mother Leona. I hope he has even forgiven me. But most of all, he's forgiven himself and that's the hardest hill to climb.

So now, as I watch his soul cross over, I know I can finally be at peace. I can reunite with Luigi and Henry, *two souls that I have yearned to see for so long.*

And as for the legend of the Woman in the River? Well, now that William and I are going to our eternal rest, I find that I no longer care how they slander my name. Let them think it was me, an Italian Marchesa who left everything behind. Let them use my name in vain.

Because if my name forces children to be a little more vigilant and parents to be less complacent with their children's safety? Well, in that case, my name does more good now as the Woman in the River than it ever did as the fallen noblewoman.

And that, also, provides my soul with eternal peace.